It was his wife, most certainly. But transformed.

The gown was a pale green, and with her light hair and fair skin she seemed almost transparent. As she came toward him he imagined he was seeing a spirit, a ghost that belonged to the house, that had been there long before he had come.

And then the light from his lamp touched the gown, and the sarcenet fabric shifted in color from silver to green again, and the silver sequins sparkled on the drape of netting that fell from her shoulder to the floor.

His friends would not call her a beauty, certainly. She was most unlike all the other women who were lauded as such. But suddenly it did not matter what his friends might say. It only mattered what he knew in his heart to be true. She looked as she was meant to look. And now that he had removed her from whatever magic realm she belonged to, he was overcome with the desire to protect her from the coarse harshness of the world around them.

* * *

Miss Winthorpe's Elopement
Harlequin® Historical #984—March 2010

Author Note

I can't point to any one place or idea that inspired me to write the story of Penny and Adam. But I started on a day when I really just wanted to sit by myself and read. That is probably why I have a book-loving heroine. There is nothing quite like the feeling of sitting down with a good book, although I can't seem to read as many as I buy. Penny's overstocked library is definitely inspired by my own.

I don't normally use pictures as inspiration, but the little china figurine in Penny's sitting room really exists. I don't own anything like it, but I wanted something that would remind me of long afternoons I spent in an aunt's living room, surrounded by "breakables." I found just the thing, searching the Internet: a figurine so fussy that it seemed the polar opposite of serious scholarship.

I hope you enjoy *Miss Winthorpe's Elopement* as much as I did.

Miss Winthorpe's ELOPEMENT

Christine Merrill

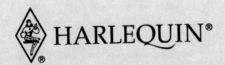
HARLEQUIN®

TORONTO • NEW YORK • LONDON
AMSTERDAM • PARIS • SYDNEY • HAMBURG
STOCKHOLM • ATHENS • TOKYO • MILAN • MADRID
PRAGUE • WARSAW • BUDAPEST • AUCKLAND

Recycling programs
for this product may
not exist in your area.

ISBN-13: 978-0-373-29584-5

MISS WINTHORPE'S ELOPEMENT

Copyright © 2008 by Christine Merrill

First North American Publication 2010

This edition published by arrangement with Harlequin Books S.A.

For questions and comments about the quality of this book please contact us at Customer_eCare@Harlequin.ca.

www.eHarlequin.com

Printed in U.S.A.

To Sean:
For doing his homework on the Greek classics.
Without you, honey, I'd have to do all my own research.

Chapter One

In the quiet of the library, Penelope Winthorpe heard the front doorbell ring, and set her book carefully aside, pushing her glasses up the bridge of her nose. She smoothed her sensible, bombazine skirt. Then she stood and strolled toward the front hall.

There was no reason to rush since hurrying would not change the results of the trip. Her brother had accused her of being too prone to impulsive actions. Seeing her hare down the hall every time the front door opened would reinforce his view that too much education and too much solitude were affecting her nerves.

But her package was two days late, and it was difficult to contain her anticipation. She rose eagerly with every knock at the door, hoping each one to be the delivery she'd been expecting.

In her mind, she was already holding the package, hearing the rustle of crisp, brown paper, running her fingers along the string that held it in place. She would cut the twine with the scissors on the hall table, and the book would be in her hands at last. She imagined she could smell the fresh ink and the paper, caress the leather of the binding, and feel the gold-embossed title under her fingertips.

And then, the best part: she would take it back to the library and cut the pages open, spread them carefully, turning each one and catching glimpses of words without really reading, not wanting to spoil the surprise, even though she knew the story, almost by heart.

At last, she would ring for tea, settle into her favourite chair by the fire, and begin to read.

It would be heaven.

When she got to the hall, her brother was sorting through a stack of letters. The post had come, but there was no sign of a package from the book seller.

'Hector, did a delivery arrive for me? I had expected it by now, but I thought perhaps it might come with the post.'

'Another book?' He sighed.

'Yes. The latest printing of *The Odyssey*.'

Her brother waved a dismissive hand. 'It came yesterday. I sent it back to the shop.'

'You did what?' She stared at him, incredulous.

'Sent it back. You already have it. I did not deem it necessary.'

'I have translations,' she corrected. 'This was in the original Greek.'

'All the more reason to send it back. I dare say the translations will be much easier for you to read.'

She took a deep breath and tried counting to ten

before speaking, to control her rash tongue. She made it almost to five before blurting, 'I do not expect to have trouble with the Greek. I read it fluently. As a matter of fact, I am planning a translation of my own. And, since I cannot translate words that are already in English, the new book will most certainly be necessary.'

Hector was looking at her as though she had sprouted a second head. 'There are many adequate translations of Homer already available.'

'But none by a woman,' she responded. 'I suspect that there are insights and subtleties I might bring to the material that will be substantially different than those already available.'

'Inferior, perhaps,' countered her brother. 'The world is not clamouring for your opinion, Penny, in case you haven't noticed.'

For a moment, the truth of that statement weighed heavy on her, but she shook it off. 'Perhaps it is because they have not yet seen what I can accomplish. I will not know until I have tried. And for that, I will need the book I ordered. Which only cost a few pounds.'

'But think of the time you would spend wasted in reading.' Hector always considered such time wasted. She remembered his discomfort in the schoolroom, and his desire to escape from it as soon as possible, when their father was ready to leave the business in his hands. That a printer had such a low opinion of books never ceased to amaze her.

'For some of us, Hector, reading is not a waste of time, but one of life's great pleasures.'

'Life is not meant to be spent in pleasure, Penelope.

I am sure, if you put your mind to it, that you can find a better way to use your time.' He looked her up and down. 'While you needn't be so frivolous as some young girls who are hellbent on matrimony, you could devote your time to higher pursuits. Helping with the poor, or the sick, perhaps.'

Penelope gnashed her teeth and set to counting. It was not that she had a distaste for charity work. It was certainly necessary. But it only showed how awkward she was around people, both rich and poor. And it served as a continual reminder to all that she was properly on the shelf, with no hope of a husband or children of her own to tend to. It felt like giving up.

Although, perhaps it was time.

And yet, she reminded herself, if she meant to give up, she could do it just as successfully at home, in front of the fire, alone except for her Homer.

This time, she made it to eight before speaking. 'It is not as though I do not wish to contribute to society,' she argued. 'But I think that what I can do for the scholarly community is just as valuable as what I might accomplish tending the ill. And I do make regular donations to the church. The help that does not come by my hand can come from my purse instead. There have been no complaints.'

Her brother glared in disapproval. 'I believe there are complaints, Penelope, although you may think that it is possible to ignore them, since they come from me. But Father has left me in charge of you and your inheritance, and so you must listen to them.'

'Until such time as I marry,' she added.

He sighed. 'We both know the unlikelihood of that, Penny. I think it is time that we accept it.'

We meant *her*, she supposed.

'It is one thing to be a bluestocking for a time. But I had hoped that you would have put such nonsense behind you by now. I do not expect you to spend your whole day at the dressmakers, or in idle gossip. But to spend no time at all on your appearance and to fill your head with opinions? And now, Greek?' He shook his own head sadly. 'Someone must put a stop to this nonsense, if you will not. No more books, Penny. At least not until you can prove to me that you are ready to grow up and accept some responsibility.'

'No books?' She felt the air leaving the room. She supposed it was as some girls might feel if their strict older brothers had said, 'No gowns. No parties. No friends.' To be denied her books was to be left companionless and unprotected in a hostile world. 'You cannot speak to me thus.'

'I believe I can.'

'Father would never have allowed it.'

'Father expected you to have started a family by now. That is why he tied your inheritance to the condition of your marriage. You have not yet found a husband. And so control of you and your money belongs to me. I will not see you fritter away the fortune that Father left to you on paper and ink.'

'A few books are hardly likely to fritter away a fortune, Hector.'

'Only a few?' He pointed to the stack on the table next to the door. 'Here are "a few books", Penny. But there are more in the dining room, and the morning room and the parlour. And your room as well, I dare say. The library is full to overflowing.'

'As it was when Father was alive, Hector. He was a man of letters. What I have added to the collection hardly amounts—'

'What you have added to the collection is hardly necessary. There are books enough to last a lifetime already in your possession.'

Perhaps if she read as slowly as her brother did… But she held her tongue and began to count again.

'And now you are buying books that you already own. It must stop, Penny. It really must. If we are to share this house in peace, I will have no more of it.'

She lost count and her temper failed her. 'Then I do not wish to live with you a moment longer.'

'I fail to see what choice you have.'

'I will marry. Someone more agreeable than you. He will be sensible and understanding, and will not begrudge me a few pounds a month for my studies.'

Hector was looking at her with pity again, but his tone was sarcastic. 'And where will you find such a paragon, dear sister? Have you forgotten the disaster of your come-out Season? Even knowing of the substantial fortune attached to it, once you opened your mouth, no one would have you. None of them was good enough for you. You are too opinionated by half. Men want a woman who will follow where they lead, not one who questions her husband's wisdom and ignores the house and the servants because she is too busy reading.'

It had been four years, and the sting of embarrassment still rose to the surface at the mention of the utter failure that had been her Season. 'But surely there is a man who wishes an intelligent wife. Someone with whom he can converse.'

Hector sniffed in disapproval. 'At such time as you find him, you are welcome to marry. But I do not see you in pursuit of such a man, nor is he in pursuit of you. Since you show no inclination to leave your desk, unless he comes stumbling into the house by mistake, it is unlikely he will find you. And thus, I am left to make your decisions for you.

'I will not push you into society, for we both know that would be hopeless. But neither will I encourage you to further education, since what you have gathered so far has caused you nothing but trouble. Good day, sister. I suggest you find something to occupy your hands, and you will see no need to busy your mind.' And he went back to reading his mail.

She was dismissed. *One, two, three…* She retreated to the stairs before she could say something that would further solidify her brother's opinions.

He was right in one thing, at least. He was entitled to make monetary decisions for her, until she could find another man to take the responsibility from him.

Not that she needed any man to do so. She was quite smart enough on her own. Smarter, she suspected, than her brother was. His hand with the family business showed none of the mastery that her father had had.

Her father loved the books he printed and bound, loved everything about the papers, the inks, and the bindings. He turned the printing of even the simplest invitation or calling card into a statement of art. And to her father, a finished volume was a masterwork.

Four, five, six… To her brother, it would never be more than profit and loss. And so, there was more loss than profit. Given a lifetime, Penny expected to see her own part in the inheritance disappear, pound by pound, to cover the shortages that would occur from his mismanagement.

Of course, it was her mention of the fact at dinner the evening before that had caused her brother's sudden interest in bringing her to heel.

Seven, eight, nine… It was unbearable. She could not live out the rest of her life under Hector's thumb, sneaking books into the house on the sly and hoping that he did not notice. To live by his rules would be impossible.

Ten.

Which left her one choice in the matter: she must marry. Even the thought of her brother's edict and the lack of books made her throat tighten in panic.

She must marry quickly.

She walked to the corner of the room and tugged the bell pull three sharp times, then turned to her wardrobe for a valise, tossing in travelling clothes from the collection of half-mourning that she had never quite managed to leave behind, although her father had been gone for two years.

In a few moments, there was a discreet knock upon the door.

'Come in, Jem.'

The senior footman looked uncomfortable, as he always did when summoned to her rooms. He had often expressed a wish that she would find a ladies' maid, or some other confidant. She had reminded him that she would do so at such time as she needed her hair dressed or a ribbon ironed. But if she needed wise counsel, she would always call upon him.

'Miss?' He stood uneasily at the door, sensing a change in the air.

'I need you to hire a carriage and prepare for travel.'

'You are going out, miss?'

She gave him a fish eye. 'I would not need a carriage, else.'

'Are we going to the book seller's, miss?' He had overheard the conversation in the hall, she suspected. And balked at doing something in direct opposition to her brother's wishes.

'No, Jem. I am not permitted to do so.'

He sagged with relief.

'So I mean to limit myself to something my brother cannot possibly object to, since he has given me permission. He wishes me to be behave as other young ladies do.'

'Very good, Miss Penny.'

'And so we are going to go and find me a husband.'

'Lost with all hands…' Adam Felkirk, Seventh Duke of Bellston, stared at the paper in front of him and watched it shake with the trembling of his hands. He tried to remind himself that the loss of almost one hundred lives far outweighed the loss of the cargo. Had the wives and families of the ship's crew been in some way prepared for the possibility of this tragedy? Perhaps. But he had certainly been foolishly unready for the fact that his investment was a risky one.

A shipment of tobacco from the Americas had seemed like a sensible plan when he had put down the money for it. The spring lambing had not gone well, and his tenants' crops were not likely to thrive in the dry weather they had been having. But tobacco was almost guaranteed to bring in more money. It was a valuable commodity, if one could pay to have it brought to England. He could sell it for a healthy profit, and the money would tide him through this year and the next.

And now, the ship was sunk, and he was ruined.

He could not help but feel that it was his own fault. God was punishing him for the mistakes of the last year, and punishing those around him as well. The burns on his brother's arm were continual memories of his faithless actions and the fire he had caused by them.

Then summer had come and the crops had failed, and he was left with the decision to waive the annual rents or throw his tenants out into the street for non-payment. When they were already hungry, what good did it do to anyone to leave them homeless as well?

And now, one hundred innocent lives were lost because he had chosen what he thought was a sensible investment.

He must face facts and tell his brother that there was nothing left. Nothing at all of what their father had left them. The house was mortgaged to the rooftop and in need of repair. There would be no income this year, and he'd gambled what was left in the bank and lost all in a risky investment.

He was out of ideas, out of money, and afraid to take another step forwards, lest it bring disaster to some unsuspecting soul that might take his side.

He ordered another whiskey. If his calculations were correct, he had enough left in his purse to get stinking drunk. And not another penny, or a way to get one for at least a year. The innkeeper might allow him credit for the room, assuming by the cut of his coat that he was good for the debt. But soon the bill would come due, and he would have to stack it with the rest, unable to pay it.

Other than his father's watch, and the signet on the fob, he had only one thing of value. The insurance on his miserable life.

His hand stopped shaking as the inevitable solution occurred to him. He was an utter failure as a duke, and a man. He had brought shame and ruin to his family. He had betrayed a friend, and been well punished for it. The gentlemanly thing to do would be to write a letter of apology and blow his brains out. Let his brother, William, have the coronet. Perhaps he could do better with it.

Of course, it would leave Will with all the debts and the additional expense of burying Adam. And the cleaning of the study from the final mess he'd made with his suicide.

But what if the present duke should die by accident, while travelling on business? Then his brother would be left with the title and a tidy sum that might cover the debts until he could find a better source of income.

Adam thought again how unjust it was that the better brain of the family had found its way into the younger son. Will had inherited wisdom, forethought and an even temper. But all the stubborn impulsiveness and pigheaded unwillingness to take advice was lodged in his own thick skull.

And Will, God love him, had not an envious or covetous bone in his body. He worshipped his older brother, although heaven knew why. He was content to see Adam make as big a mess as possible of the whole thing, never offering a word of criticism.

But no more. His brother would make a fine duke. Let Will step up and do his part to keep the estate solvent, for Adam was more than sick of trying.

But it was up to Adam to step out of the way and allow his William to come forward and take his place.

Adam set down the newspaper. He was resolved. A simple accident would solve many problems, if he had the nerve to follow through. But how best to go about it?

He ordered another whisky. As he drank, he felt the glow in his head fogging rational thought, and numbing the pain of the failure. And realised he was well on the way to the first step in his plan. Raise enough Dutch courage to do the deed, and create the level of befuddlement in his body to convince anyone that cared to ask that this was an unfortunate accident, and not a deliberate act. He finished his drink and ordered another, staying the hand of the barman. 'Leave the bottle.'

The duke could hear the faint rumble of the coaches entering and leaving the busy courtyard. He imagined the slippery cobbles under his expensive boots, and how easy it might be to fall. And the great horses with their heavy hooves, and even heavier carriage wheels…

It would not be a pleasant death. But he doubted that any death was pleasant, when it came down to the fact.

This would at least be timely, and easy enough to arrange. He poured himself another stiff whisky. He might be thought drunken and careless. But many knew him to be that already. At least they would not think him a suicidal coward.

Very well, then.

He took one final drink. Stood and felt the world tipping under his feet. Very good, indeed. He doubted he could make too many steps. He dropped the last of his coin on the table, turned to the tavern keeper and offered an unsteady bow. 'Good evening to you, sir.'

And goodbye.

He worked his way toward the door, bumping several patrons along the way and apologising profusely, before he made it through the open door of the inn.

He could hear a carriage approaching, and deliberately looked in the opposite direction, into the sun. Now he was blind, as well as drunk. All the better, for his nerve could not fail if he could not see what was coming.

The sound was getting louder and louder and he waited until he could feel the faint trembling in the ground that told him the coach was near.

Then he started forward, ignoring the calls of the coachmen.

'Here, sir. Watch where you are going.'

'I say, look out!'

'Oh, dear God!'

And his foot slipped from under him, sending him face down in front of the approaching horses.

Chapter Two

Penelope felt the steady rocking of the carriage, but the rhythm did nothing to lull the sense of dread growing in her. They had been travelling north at a steady pace toward Scotland, stopping at inns and taverns to dine or pass the night. And yet she was no nearer to her goal than when she had been sitting in front of the fire at home.

Jem's misgivings had eased only slightly, once he realised that he was not expected to be the groom. 'You cannot hire a husband as you would hire a coach, Miss Penny.'

'How hard can it be?' Penny announced, with an optimism that she hoped would carry her through the trip. 'I think disappointments in the past were the fault of expectations on the part of myself and the gentlemen involved. I wished a soulmate and they wished a biddable female. I shall never be biddable, and the fact was emphasised by the surrounding crowd of prettier, more agreeable young ladies. After the lack of success in London, I am willing to accept that there will not be a soulmate in the offing.'

The footman stared at her, as if to say it was no concern of his, one way or the other.

She continued. 'However, if I mean to hire a man to do a job of work? Times are hard, Jem. As we go further north, there will be many men seeking employment. I will find one and make my offer.'

Jem could hold his tongue no longer. 'I hardly think that marriage should be considered a chore, miss.'

'My brother assures me often enough that marriage to *me* is likely to be such. And that is just how I mean to phrase it to any worthy gentleman I might find. It will be the simplest of jobs, really. He has but to sign some papers, and spend a few weeks in my presence to pacify my brother. I will pay him amply for his time. And I will require nothing in the way of marital obligations. Not sobriety, or fidelity, or drastic change in lifestyle. He can do just as he pleases, as long as he is willing to marry.'

'A man is not likely to be so easily managed as that, miss.' His tone was warning, but the meaning was lost on her.

'I fail to see why not. It is doubtful that he will have any designs upon my person. Look at me, Jem, and tell me honestly that you expect me to be fighting off the forced affections of some man, if he has freedom and enough money for any woman he wishes.'

The footman looked doubtful.

'But I have brought you along to protect my honour, should my surmise be incorrect,' she assured him.

The elderly footman was not mollified. 'But when you marry, the money will no longer be in your control. It will belong to your husband.' Jem gestured to fill the empty air with scenarios, all of which foretold doom.

'I have no control of the money now,' Penny reminded him. 'If there is a chance that I can find a husband who is less resolute than my brother has become, then it is well worth the risk. I will need to act fast, and think faster. But I dare say I will find a way to take the reins of the relationship before my intended knows what I am about.'

He was not convinced. 'And if the choice proves disastrous?'

'We shall cross that bridge when we come to it.' She glanced out the window at the change in scenery. 'Will we be stopping soon? I fear we are getting near to Scotland, and I had hoped to find someone by now.'

Jem signalled the driver to stop at the next inn, and Penny crossed her fingers. 'It will help if I can find a man who is slow of wit and amiable in nature. If he is given to drink? All the better. Then I shall allow him his fill of it, and he will be too content to bother with me.'

Jem looked disapproving. 'You mean to keep the poor man drunk so that you may do as you will.'

She sniffed. 'I mean to offer him the opportunity to drink. It is hardly my fault if he is unable to resist.'

Jem rolled his eyes.

The carriage was slowing, and when she looked out the window, she could see that they were approaching an inn. She leaned back against her seat and offered a silent prayer that this stop would be the one where she met with success. The other places she had tried were either empty of custom or filled with the sort of rugged brawlers who looked no more willing to allow her freedom than her brother was. Her plan was a wild one, of course. But there were many miles to travel, and she only needed to find one likely candidate for it to prove successful.

And surely there was one man, between London and Gretna, who was in as desperate a state as she. She had but to find him.

Suddenly, the carriage jerked to a stop, and rattled and shook as the horses reared in front of it. She reached out and caught the leather strap at her side, clinging to it to keep her seat. The driver was swearing as he fought to control the beasts and shouting to someone in front of them as things began to settle to something akin to normal. She shot a worried look at Jem in the seat across from her.

He held up a warning hand, indicating that she keep her place, and opened the door, stepping out of the carriage and out of sight to check on the disturbance.

When he did not return, she could not resist, and left the carriage to see for herself.

They had stopped before the place she had expected, several yards short of the inn. But it was easy to understand the reason. There was a body, sprawled face down in the muck at the feet of the horses, which were still shying nervously. The driver held them steady, as Jem bent to examine the unconscious man in the road.

He appeared to be a gentleman, from what little she could see. The back of his coat was well cut, and stretched to cover broad shoulders. Although the buff of the breeches was stained with dirt from the road, she was sure that they had been new and clean earlier in the day.

Jem reached a hand to the man's shoulder and shook him gently, then with more force. When there was no response, he rolled the inert figure on to his back.

The dark hair was mussed, but stylish, the face clean shaven, and the long slender fingers of his hands showed none of the marks of hard work. Not a labourer or common ruffian. A gentleman, most certainly. She supposed it was too much to hope that he was a scholar. More likely a rake, so given over to dissolution that, left to his own devices, he was likely to drink himself to death before they reached the border.

She smiled. 'He is almost too perfect. Put him into the coach at once, Jem.'

Her servant looked at her as though she'd gone mad.

She shrugged. 'I was trusting to fortune to make my decision for me. I hoped that she would throw a man in my path, and she has done just that. You must admit, it is very hard to doubt the symbolic nature of this meeting.'

Jem stared down at the man, and nudged his shoulder. 'Here, sir. Wake up.'

His eyes opened, and she could not help but notice the heavy fringe of lashes that hid the startlingly blue irises. The colour was returning to the high-boned, pale cheeks. He looked up into the blinding sun, and released a sigh. 'There was no pain. I had thought…' Then the man looked past Jem, and smiled up at her. 'Are you an angel?'

She snorted. 'Are you foxed?'

'It depends,' he muttered. 'If I am alive, then I am foxed. But if I am dead? Then I am euphoric. And you—' he pointed a long white finger '—are an angel.'

'Either way, I doubt you should lie here in the road, sir. Would you care to join me in my carriage? I am on a journey.'

'To heaven.' He smiled.

She thought of Gretna Green, which might be quite lovely, but fell far short of Elysium. 'We are all journeying towards heaven, are we not? But some of us are closer than others.'

He nodded, and struggled to his feet. 'Then I must stay close to you if the Lord has sent you to be my guide.'

Jem tossed the man a handkerchief, and he stared at it in confusion. Finally, the servant took it back, wiped the man's face and hands and brushed off his coat and breeches. He turned the man's head to get his attention and said slowly, 'You are drunk, sir. And you have fallen in a coach yard. Are you alone? Or are there friends to aid you in your predicament?'

The man laughed. 'I doubt any of my friends could help me find my way to heaven, for they have chosen a much darker path.' He gestured around him. 'None of them is here, in any case. I am very much alone.'

Jem looked disgusted. 'We cannot just leave you here. You might wander into the road again, if there is no one to stop you. And you seem harmless enough. Do you promise, if we take you along with us, not to bother the young mistress?'

'Take liberties with such a divine creature?' He

cocked his head to the side. 'I would not think of it, sir, on my immortal soul, and my honour as a gentleman.'

Jem threw his hands in the air and stared at Penelope. 'If you mean to have him, miss, I will not stop you. He appears to be a drunken idiot, but not particularly dangerous.'

The man nodded in enthusiastic agreement.

'Your brother will have my head if I'm wrong, of course.'

'My brother will not hear of it. He will not take you back, Jem, once he realises that you have helped me. You had best stay with me and hope for a favourable outcome. If we succeed, I will reward you well for your part in this.'

Jem helped her and the man back into the body of the coach, climbed in and shut the doors behind him. They set off again, and the man across from her looked surprised by the movement, before settling back into the squabs.

She smiled at him. 'I don't believe I asked your name, sir.'

'I don't believe you did.' He grinned at her. 'Adam Felkirk. And what am I to call you?

'Penelope Winthorpe.'

'I am not dead, then?' He seemed vaguely disappointed.

'No. Are you in some sort of trouble?'

He frowned. 'I most certainly am. Or will be, if I wake sober in the morning.' He smiled again. 'But for now, I am numb and free from care.'

'Suppose I could promise you enough brandy that you need never to be sober again?'

He grinned. 'At the moment, it is a most attractive proposition.'

'Brandy, Jem. I know you have some. Give it to Mr Felkirk.'

Jem looked horrified that his mistress would force him to acknowledge the flask in his pocket, and even worse, that she would require him to part with it. But he gave it over to the man in the seat next to him.

Felkirk nodded his thanks. 'If she is an angel, then you, sir, are a saint.' He raised the flask in salute and drank.

She examined him. He had an insubstantial quality. Harmless and friendly. She had feared that Jem spoke the truth when he had said that a real man might be more difficult to manage than the one she had imagined for her purpose. But Adam Felkirk seemed easy enough.

'Thank you for your kind words, Mr Felkirk. And if you wish more brandy, then do not hesitate to inform me.'

He smiled and drank again, then offered the flask to her.

She took it and considered it for a moment, before deciding that drink would not help her gain the courage to speak. 'But that is not all.' She tried a smile that was welcoming and friendly, since seduction seemed inappropriate for her purpose. 'You could have fine clothes as well. And a pretty mistress. Money always in your pocket, and a chance to do just as you please, in all things, at all times.'

He grinned at her, and she was taken aback by the whiteness of his smile. 'You truly are an angel, darling. And leading me to a heaven most suited for a man of my tastes. I had imagined something more pious.' He pulled a face. 'Downy clouds, flowing robes. Harps and whatnot. But heaven, as you describe it, sounds more like a fine evening in London.'

'If that is what you wish, you may have it. Whenever you want. I can relieve you of all cares. But first, you must do one thing for me.' She handed the flask back to him again.

He took it and drank deeply. 'As I suspected—it was far too pleasant to be heaven. And you are not an angel, but a demon, come for my soul.' He laughed. 'But I fear the devil might have that already, so what can I do?'

'Nothing so dire.' She smiled again, and told him her plan.

It was not at all clear that the truth was reaching him. He was smiling back at her, and nodding at the appropriate times. But with each sip of brandy, his eyes lost a little of their glitter. And, as often as not, he looked out the window rather than at her.

When she reached the word marriage, his eyes focused for a moment, and he opened his mouth. But it was as though he'd forgotten what it was he meant to say. He looked absently at her, then shrugged and took another drink, and his smile returned.

The carriage pulled to a stop, and Jem hopped down to open the door, announcing that they had arrived at Gretna Green. She stared at the man across from her, 'Do you agree to my terms, Mr Felkirk?'

'Call me Adam, my dear.' He was staring at her with increased intensity, and for a moment she feared that he meant a closer relationship than she intended. And then he said, 'I am sorry, but I seem to have forgotten your name. Oh, well. No matter. Why are we stopping?'

'We are in Gretna Green.'

'There was something you wanted me to do, wasn't there?'

'Sign a licence?' she prompted.

'Of course! Let us do that, then. And then we shall have some more brandy.' He seemed to think it was all jolly fun, and reached for the door handle, nearly losing his balance as Jem opened it in front of him. The servant caught his elbow and helped him down out of the coach, before reaching a hand up to help Penny.

When they were on the ground together, Adam offered his arm to her. She took it, and found herself leading him, steadying him, more than he ever could her. But he went along, docile as a lamb.

She led him to the blacksmith, and listened as Jem explained to the man what was required.

'Well, git on wi' it, then. I have horses ta shoe.' He looked critically at Penny. 'Da ya mean ta ha' him?'

'I do,' she said formally, as though it mattered.

'Yer sure? He's a drunkard. They cause no end a trouble.'

'I wish to marry him, all the same.'

'And you, sir. Will ya ha' the lady?'

'Marriage?' Adam grinned. 'Oh, I say. That is a lark, isn't it?' He looked down at her. 'I cannot remember quite why, but I must have intended it, or I wouldn't be in Scotland. Very well. Let us be married.'

'Done. Yer married. Na off with you. I ha' work ta do.' He turned back to his horses.

'That is all?' Penny asked in surprise. 'Is there a paper to be signed? Something that will prove what we have done?'

'If ya wanted a licence, ya coulda staid on yer own side o' the border, lass.'

'But I must have something to show to my brother, and the solicitors of course. Can you not provide for us, sir?'

'I canna write, so there is verra little I ca' do for ya, less ya need the carriage mended, or the horse shoed.'

'I will write it myself, then. Jem, run back to the carriage and find me some paper, and a pen and ink.'

The smith was looking at her as if she were daft, and Adam laughed, patted the man on the back and whispered something in his ear, offering him a drink from the brandy flask, which the Scot refused.

Penny stared down at the paper before her. What did she need to record? A marriage had taken place. The participants. The location. The date.

There was faint hammering in the background and the hiss of hot metal as it hit the water.

Their names, of course. She spelled Felkirk as she expected it to be, hoping that she was not showing her ignorance of her new husband by the misspelling of her new surname.

She glanced down at the paper. It looked official, in a sad sort of way. Better than returning with nothing to show her brother. She signed with a bold hand and indicated a spot where Jem could sign as witness.

Her new husband returned to her side from the forge, where he had been watching the smithy. He held a hand out to her. 'Now here, angel, is the trick

if you want to be legal. Not married without a ring, are
you?' He was holding something small and dark
between the fingers of his hand. 'Give over.' He
reached for her.

'I think your signature is all that is needed. And that
of the smith, of course.' She smiled hopefully at the
smith. 'You will be compensated, sir, for the trouble.'

At the mention of compensation, he took the pen and
made his mark at the bottom of the paper.

'Here, here, sir.' Her husband took another drink, in
the man's honour. 'And to my wife.' He drank again.
'Your Grace.'

She shook her head. 'Now, you are mistaking me for
someone else, Adam. Perhaps it would be best to leave
off the brandy for a time.'

'You said I could have all I wanted. And so I shall.'
But there was no anger as he said it. 'Your hand,
madam.' He took her left hand and slipped something
on to the ring finger, then reached for the pen.

She glanced down. The smith had twisted a horse-
shoe nail into a crude semblance of a ring, and her hand
was heavily weighted with it. Further proof that she had
truly been to Scotland, since the X of the smith held no
real meaning.

Adam signed with a flourish, beside her own name.
'We need to seal it as well. Makes it look more official.'
He snatched the candle from the table and dripped a clot
of the grease at the bottom of the paper, and pulled out
his watch fob, which held a heavy gold seal. 'There. As
good as anything in Parliament.' He grinned down at the
paper and tipped the flask up for another drink.

She stared at the elegant signature above the wax. 'Adam Felkirk, Duke of Bellston.'

'At your service, madam.' He bowed deeply, and the weight of his own head overbalanced him. Then he pitched forward, striking his head on the corner of the table, to fall unconscious at her feet.

Chapter Three

Adam regained consciousness, slowly. It was a mercy, judging by the way he felt when he moved his head. He remembered whisky. A lot of whisky. Followed by brandy, which was even more foolish. And his brain and body remembered it as well, and were punishing him for the consumption. His head throbbed, his mouth was dry as cotton, and his eyes felt full of sand.

He moved slightly. He could feel bruises on his body. He reached up and probed the knot forming on his temple. From a fall.

And there had been another fall. In the coach yard.

Damn it. He was alive.

He closed his eyes again. If he'd have thought it through, he'd have recognised his mistake. Carriages were slowing down when they reached the inn yard. The one he'd stepped in front of had been able to stop in time to avoid hitting him.

'Waking up, I see.'

Adam raised his head and squinted into the unfamiliar room at the man sitting beside the bed. 'Who the devil are you?'

The man was at least twenty years his senior, but unbent by age, and powerfully built. He was dressed as a servant, but showed no subservience, for he did not answer the question. 'How much do you remember of yesterday, your Grace?'

'I remember falling down in front of an inn.'

'I see.' The man said nothing more.

'Would you care to enlighten me? Or am I to play yes and no, until I can suss out the details?'

'The carriage you stepped in front of belonged to my mistress.'

'I apologise,' he said, not feeling the least bit sorry. 'I hope she was not unduly upset.'

'On the contrary. She considered it a most fortunate circumstance. And I assure you, you were conscious enough to agree to what she suggested, even if you do not remember it. We did not learn your identity until you'd signed the licence.'

'Licence?'

'You travelled north with us, your Grace. To Scotland.'

'Why the devil would I do that?' Adam lowered his voice, for the volume of his own words made the pounding in his skull more violent.

'You went to Gretna, to a blacksmith.'

He shook his head, and realised immediately that it had been a mistake to try such drastic movement. He remained perfectly still and attempted another answer.

'It sounds almost as if you are describing an elopement. Did I stand in witness for someone?'

The servant held the paper before him, and he could see his shaky signature at the bottom, sealed with his fob and a dab of what appeared to be candle wax. Adam lunged for it, and the servant stepped out of the way.

His guts heaved at the sudden movement, leaving him panting and sweating as he waited for the rocking world to subside.

'Who?' he croaked.

'Is your wife?' completed the servant.

'Yes.'

'Penelope Winthorpe. She is a printer's daughter, from London.'

'Annulment.'

'Before you suggest it to her, let me apprise you of the facts. She is worth thirty thousand a year and has much more in her bank. If I surmise correctly, you were attempting to throw yourself under the horses when we met you. If the problem that led you to such a rash act was monetary, it was solved this morning.'

He fell back into the pillows and struggled to remember any of the last day. There was nothing there. Apparently, he had fallen face down in the street and found himself an heiress to marry.

Married to the daughter of a tradesman. How could he have been so foolish? His father would be horrified to see the family brought to such.

Of course, his father had been dead for many years. His opinions in the matter were hardly to be considered. And considering that the result of his own careful planning was a sunk ship, near bankruptcy, and attempted suicide, a hasty marriage to some rich chit was not so great a disaster.

And if the girl were lovely and personable?

He relaxed. She must be, if he had been so quick to marry her. He must have been quite taken with her, although he did not remember the fact. There had to be a reason that he had offered for her, other than just the money, hadn't there?

It was best to speak with her, before deciding on a course of action. He gestured to the servant. 'I need a shave. And have someone draw water for a bath. Then I will see this mistress of yours, and we will discuss what is to become of her.'

An hour later, Penelope hesitated at the door to the duke's bedroom, afraid to enter and trying in vain to convince herself that she had any right to be as close to him as she was.

The illogic of her former actions rang in her ears. What had she been thinking? She must have been transported with rage to have come up with such a foolhardy plan. Now that she was calm enough to think with a clear head, she must gather her courage and try to undo the mess she'd made. Until the interview was over, the man was her husband. Why should she not visit him in his rooms?

But the rest of her brain screamed that this man was not her husband. This was the Duke of Bellston, peer of the realm and leading figure in Parliament, whose eloquent speeches she had been reading in *The Times* scant weeks ago. She had heartily applauded his opinions and looked each day for news about him, since he seemed, above all others, to offer wise and reasoned governance. As she'd scanned the papers for any mention of him, her brother had remarked it was most like a woman to romanticise a public figure.

But she had argued that she admired Bellston for his ideas. The man was a political genius, one of the great minds of the age, which her brother might have noticed, had he not been too mutton-headed to concern himself with current affairs. There was nothing at all romantic about it, for it was not the man itself she admired, but the positions he represented.

And it was not as if the papers had included a caricature of the duke that she was swooning over. She had no idea how he might look in person. So she had made his appearance up in her head out of whole cloth. By his words, she had assumed him to be an elder statesmen, with grey hair, piercing eyes and a fearsome intellect. Tall and lean, since he did not appear from his speeches to be given to excesses, in diet or spirit.

If she were to meet him, which of course she never would, she would wish only to engage him in discourse, and question him on his views, perhaps offering a few of her own. But it would never happen, for what would such a great man want with her and her opinions?

She would never in a million years have imagined him as a handsome young noble, or expected to find him stone drunk and face down in the street where he had very nearly met his end under her horse. And never in a hundred million years would she expect to find herself standing in front of his bedchamber.

She raised her hand to knock, but before she could make contact with the wood, she heard his voice from within. 'Enter, if you are going to, or return to your rooms. But please stop lurking in the hallway.'

She swallowed annoyance along with her fear, opened the door, and stepped into the room.

Adam Felkirk was sitting beside the bed, and made no effort to rise as she came closer. His seat might as well have been a throne as a common wooden chair, for he held his position with the confidence of a man who could buy and sell the inn and the people in it, and not think twice about the bills. He stared at her, unsmiling, and even though he looked up into her eyes it felt as though he were looking down upon her.

The man in front of her was obviously a peer. How could she have missed the fact yesterday?

Quite easily, she reminded herself. A day earlier he could manage none of the hauteur he was displaying now. Unlike some men, the excess of liquor made him amiable. Drunkenness had relaxed his resolute posture and softened his features.

Not that the softness had made them any more appealing. Somehow she had not noticed what a handsome man she had chosen, sober and clean, shaved and in fresh linen. She felt the irresistible pull the moment she looked at him. He was superb. High cheekbones and pale skin no longer flushed with whisky. Straight nose, thick dark hair. And eyes of the deepest blue, so clear that to look into them refreshed the soul. And knowing the mind that lay behind them, she grew quite weak. There was a hint of sensuality in the mouth, and she was carnally aware of the quirk of the lips when he looked at her, and the smile behind them.

And now he was waiting for her to speak. 'Your Grace…' she faltered.

'It is a day too late to be so formal, madam.' His voice, now that it was not slurred, held a tone of command that she could not resist.

She dropped a curtsy.

He sneered. 'Leave off with that, immediately. If it is meant to curry favour, it is not succeeding. Your servant explained some of what happened, while he was shaving me. It seems this marriage was all your idea, and none of mine?'

'I am sorry. I had no idea who you were.'

He examined her closely, as though she were a bug on a pin. 'You expect me to believe that you were unaware of my title when you waylaid me to Scotland?'

'Completely. I swear. You were injured in the street before my carriage. I was concerned for your safety.'

'And so you married me. Such a drastic rescue was not necessary.'

'I meant to marry someone. It was the intent of the trip.'

'And when you found a peer, lying helpless in the street—'

'As I told you before, I had no idea of your title. And I could hardly have left you alone. Suppose you had done harm to yourself?'

There was a sharp intake of breath from the man across the table from her and she hoped that she had not insulted him by the implication.

'I am sorry. But you seemed insensible. You were in a vulnerable state.'

'And you took advantage of it.'

She hung her head. 'I have no defence against that accusation.' She held out the mock licence to him. 'But I am prepared to offer you your freedom. No one knows what has occurred between us. Here is the only record of it. The smith that witnessed could not read the words upon it, and never inquired your name. I will not speak of it, nor will my servant. You have but to throw it on the fire and you are a free man.'

'As easy as that.' The sarcasm in his voice was plain. 'You will never trouble me again. You do not intend to reappear, when I choose to marry again, and wave a copy of this in my face. You will never announce to my bride that she has no legal right to wed me?'

'Why should I?' she pleaded. 'I hold no malice towards you. It is you that hold me in contempt, and I richly deserve it. Do I wish to extort money from you? Again, the answer would be no. I have ample enough fortune to supply my needs. I do not seek yours.'

He was looking at her as though he could not believe what he was hearing. 'You truly do not understand the gravity of what you have done. I cannot simply throw this on the fire and pretend nothing has happened. Perhaps you can. But I signed it, with my true name and title, and sealed it as well. Drunk or sober, for whatever reason, the result is the same. I am legally bound to you. If my name is to mean anything to me, I cannot ignore the paper in front of me.'

He stared at the licence, and his eyes looked bleak.

'You are right that no one need know if I destroy it. But
I would know of it. If we had been in England, it would
be a Fleet marriage and would mean nothing. But by the
laws of Scotland, we are man and wife. To ignore this
and marry again without a formal annulment would be
bigamy. It matters not to me that I am the only one who
knows the truth. I cannot behave thus and call myself a
man of honour.'

She willed herself not to cry, for tears would do no
good. They would make her look even more foolish
than she already did. 'Then you shall have your annulment, your Grace. In any way that will suit you. I am
sorry that scandal cannot be avoided, but I will take all
the blame in the matter.'

'Your reputation will be in ruins.'

She shook her head. 'A spotless reputation has in no
way balanced my shortcomings thus far. What harm
can scandal do me?'

'Spotless?' He was eyeing her again. 'Most young
girls with spotless reputations have no need to flee to
Scotland for a hasty marriage to a complete stranger.'

'You thought I was…' Oh, dear lord. He thought she
was with child, which made her behaviour seem even
more sordid and conniving then it already was. 'No.
That is not the problem. Not at all. My circumstances
are…' she sought a word '…unusual.'

'Unusual circumstances?' He arched his eyebrows,
leaned back and folded his arms. 'Tell me of them. If
we have eliminated fortune hunting, blackmail and the
need to find a father for your bastard, then I am out of
explanations for your behaviour.'

He was staring at her, waiting. And she looked down into those very blue eyes, and, almost against her will, began to speak. She told him of her father. And her brother. The conditions of her inheritance. The foolishness over the book. 'And so, I decided that I must marry. It did not really matter to whom. If I could find someone on the way to Scotland... And then you fell in front of the carriage.'

He was looking at her most curiously. 'Surely you hoped for better than a total stranger.'

'Once, perhaps. But now I hope only for peace and quiet, and to be surrounded by my books.'

'But a girl with the fortune you claim...'

It was her turn to sneer at him. 'A plain face and disagreeable nature have managed to offset any financial advantages a marriage to me might offer. Only the most desperate would be willing to put up with me, for I can be most uncooperative when crossed.

'Since I know from experience that I will refuse to be led by my husband in all things, I sought someone I could control.' She looked at him and shook her head. 'And I failed, most dreadfully. In my defence, you were most biddable while intoxicated.'

He laughed, and it surprised her. 'Once you had found this biddable husband, what did you mean to do with him?'

'Gain control of my inheritance. Retire to my library and allow my husband to do as he chose in all things not pertaining to me.'

'In all things not pertaining to you.' He was staring at her again, and it occurred to her the things he might expect from a woman who was his wife. Suddenly, the room felt unaccountably warm.

She dropped her eyes from his. 'I did not wish for intimacy. But neither did I expect fidelity. Or sobriety. Or regular hours, or even attendance in the same house. I had hoped for civility, of course. But affection was not required. I did not wish to give over all of my funds, but I certainly do not need all of them for myself. If they remain with my brother, in time I will have nothing at all. I have thirty thousand a year. I should suspect that half would be more than enough for most gentlemen to entertain themselves.'

Again, there was an intake of breath from the man across from her. 'Suppose the gentleman needed more.'

'More?' She blinked back at him.

'One hundred and fifty thousand, as soon as possible.'

One hundred and fifty thousand. The number was mind-boggling, but she considered it, doing the maths in her head. 'I should not think it would be a problem. I have savings. And I do not need much to live on. While it will reduce my annual income considerably, it will leave more than enough for my needs.'

He studied her even more intently, got up and walked slowly around her, considering her from several angles. Then he returned to his chair. 'If I go to your brother and present myself as your husband, which indeed I am, then you would give me one hundred and fifty thousand pounds and the freedom to do as I wish with it?'

'It is only money. But it is my money, and I can do as I will.' She looked back into his eyes, searching for anything that might give her a clue as to his true nature, and hoping that it aligned in some small way with the man who had written such wonderful speeches. 'I should as soon see you have it as my brother, for I am most angry with him. You may have as much money as you need. If you agree to my other conditions, of course.'

He met her gaze without flinching. 'Why would I have to do that? Now that I am your husband, I can do as I please with all the money. You are a woman, and lost all say in the matter when you were foolish enough to wed a stranger.'

'There was the flaw in my plan,' she admitted. 'I expected to find a man slower in wit than the one I seem to have married. A drunken fool would be easy enough to gull. I could distract him with pleasures of the flesh. By the time he sobered enough to realise the extent of his good fortune, I meant to have the majority of my assets converted to cash and secured against him.'

She looked as closely at him as he had at her. 'But you are likely to know better. And I have given you the licence that proves your right to control my money, should you choose to exercise it. In truth, I am as much at your mercy now as you were at mine yesterday.'

There was a flicker of something in his eyes that she could not understand.

She said, 'You say you are a man of honour. And so I must appeal to your better nature. If you wish it, you may destroy the paper in front of you or we can go to London and seek a formal annulment.

'Or we can go directly to my bankers, and you can

take control of the fortune, which is your right as my husband. If so, I beg you to allow me some measure of freedom, and the time and money necessary to pursue my studies. The choice is yours.'

She thought to dip her head in submission, and decided against it. She waited in silence, watching for some sign of what he might say next. And the look in his eyes changed gradually from one of suspicion, to speculation, to calculation and eventually to something she thought might be avarice. He was thinking of the money. And what he might do with it, God help her.

It was a day too late to inquire what that might be. She had found the man, drunk as a lord in a public place. Who knew what vices he might be capable of? If she had not cared to discover this yesterday, it did no good to care now. And if his lechery and drunkenness were strong enough to run through the whole of her money, then it would prove to her brother just how foolish she was.

At last, he spoke. 'When you found me, I was near the end of my rope. An investment that should have returned enough to tide me and my estate through the coming year had failed, utterly. I have responsibilities. People are depending on me for their welfare. And I am destitute.

'Or was, until you appeared and offered me this opportunity. What I need to do may take a larger portion of your money than you had hoped to part with. But I hope it will be a temporary loss. My land is fertile most years, and returns more than enough to live in luxury. Had I not gambled with the profits, hoping for an increase, I would not be in need of your help.'

Gambling? Although it did not please her, it made perfect sense. Many men of considerable wealth lost all over a green baize table. She could but hope that she might hide some of the money from him, or perhaps, through sound advice, she might prevent him from making a similar mistake in the future.

He was waiting for some response on her part, and she gave him a faint nod of understanding.

He continued. 'In exchange, you shall be a duchess, which will make it possible to do largely as you please in all things. No one will dare to question your actions or your spending, least of all me. If you do not have cash in hand, no one will deny you credit. The bills will come to me, to be paid at such time as we have the funds for them.'

Doing business on credit went against her nature. But the prospect of freedom beckoned, and hope flared in her. 'And my studies?'

'If you do not wish to question my diversions, then what right would I have to question yours?'

As her husband? He would have every right in the world. But he was being most reasonable about things, so she held her tongue on the literalities. 'I doubt we would have much in common—in the matter of diversions, I mean.'

He nodded. 'Quite possibly not. We might live comfortably as strangers, although in the same house.' There was no sense of remorse as he said it. 'But I see no reason that we cannot succeed at it. As long as we have no intention of impeding each other's pleasure, we might manage well together. Certainly better than some couples I know who seem bent on ensuring their spouse's misery.'

It seemed so cold, when stated thus. But her new husband seemed content with it. He did not care that she wished to be alone with her books. And looking at his full lips and the seductive light in his blue eyes, she suspected the less she knew about his activities when he was not in Parliament, the happier she would be.

She ventured, 'It sounds most pleasant when you describe it thus.' Which was not precisely true. 'And very much what I was hoping for.' Which was. It was exactly what she had hoped for, and she must not forget the fact.

He smiled in return, although there was a frozen quality to his face that made her unsure. 'Very well, then.' He reached out a hand to her, and she stared at it for a moment before offering him her own. He took it and shook. 'We are in agreement. Let us hope that this union will prove mutually beneficial.'

'Will you be ready to start for London today?'

He started at the impertinence of her request. He was not accustomed to having another set his schedule.

She hesitated. 'I admit to being most eager to bring the news of my marriage to my brother. And my bankers, of course.'

He remembered the money, and his resistance to her suggestion evaporated. 'Today would suit me nicely. Have your footman prepare the carriage.' He nodded in such a way that she knew the interview was at an end and she was dismissed.

Adam watched his new wife exit the room and sank back into his chair, exhausted. What in God's name had he just agreed to? He'd sunk so low as to marry a cit's daughter, just to get her money.

And a cool voice at the back of his head reminded him that it was better than his first plan, if it meant that he could be alive to correct his mistake and rebuild his fortune. He had been given a second chance and would make the most of it. There would be money in the bank before his creditors noticed that there had been an absence. And by next year, the drought would be over, the coffers refilling and the present state of penury no more than a bad dream.

And he would be a married man. What was he to do with—he struggled to remember her name— Penelope Winthorpe?

He shook his head. She was Penelope Felkirk now. And there was nothing to be done, according to her. She wished to be left alone.

He was more than willing to grant her wish. He could not very well parade her in front of his friends as the new duchess. He'd be a laughing stock.

He immediately felt guilty for his pride. He'd be a laughing stock in any case, knowing his circle, who often found the humour in the misfortunes of others. Let them laugh. It would not matter, if he managed to save the estate.

But it pained him that they might laugh at her, as well, with her unfashionable clothes, her spectacles and outlandish ideas. To what purpose did the world need another translation of Homer? The majority had had more than enough of that story, by the time they'd left the schoolroom. And yet she was still worrying over it.

But he could find no indication that she meant him harm, by picking him up out of the street. In truth, she had saved his life. And her money would save his land as well.

What would people think of it? She was most obviously not his sort, in temperament or in birth. She was nothing like the ladies of the *ton* that he usually chose as companions. The world expected him to marry someone more like Clarissa Colton: beautiful, worldly, and with wit that cut like a razor. He shuddered.

Perhaps it told him something of his true mental state that he had married Clare's opposite. Penelope Winthorpe's clothes were without style, and her manner was bookish and hesitant. And her looks?

He shook his head. She'd called herself plain, but it was not truly accurate a definition. Plainness implied a commonality with the norm. A face unmemorable. And that did not describe his new wife.

Her looks…were disturbing. Her hair was too pale, almost white. Her skin as well, from too much time spent indoors with her books. And her spectacles hid eyes that were bright and far too observant. He wanted to know what she saw when she looked at him, for she had been studying him most intently. It was like being pierced to the soul, when her eye had held his. A gimlet, not a razor.

The intelligence in that gaze was daunting. And in her words as well. He'd have expected it from another man, but to hear such reasonable behaviour from a woman? There had been no nonsense. No tears behind the lashes. No attempt to appeal to him with her frailty. Their interview had been a frank meeting of intellectual equals.

Her presence had been both calming and stimulating. The combination made him uneasy. It was far too much to take before one had had one's morning tea.

But it shouldn't matter, he reminded himself. He needed nothing more from her than her money, and she needed nothing from him but his name. There would be scant little time staring into those disquieting eyes over breakfast. If she did not care for his title, then she need not concern herself with society, after the briefest introduction. And he would be spared the expenses of time or money that were involved in the keeping of a wife in the height of fashion.

And it dawned on him that there were other responsibilities in the taking of a wife that had nothing to do with the purchase of jewels and the redecoration of the manor.

There should be children.

He thought of her eyes again, and imagined a brood of little eyes following him with that same direct stare: dangerously clever children with insatiable curiosity. The prospect intrigued him, but it was not something he was likely to experience, if their current plan went forwards.

It came as somewhat of a relief to know that the title could follow another branch of the family tree. He had his brother as heir. That had been a fine plan yesterday. And if not William, then perhaps William would marry and have sons of his own. Good-tempered and intelligent children, just like their father. Any of those might do for the next duke.

Very well, then. He would take her back to London, or let her take him. And if what she said was true, he would sort out the money, right enough. And once she and her books were safely stowed at Bellston, then he could return to his comfortable old life. They would live, happily ever after, as was told in folk tales.

Just not with each other.

Chapter Four

The carriage ride to London was nothing like the one to Gretna. The trip outbound had been more excitement than misgiving, since she was convinced of the soundness of her plan and the immediate improvement it would bring to her life.

But now that she had succeeded, she found it most disquieting. Jem had been relegated to a seat beside the driver, leaving her alone with her new husband with a morose shake of the head that showed no confidence in a brighter future.

The man seated across from her was not the drunkard she had rescued on the way to Scotland. That man had been relaxed and friendly. His posture was familiar, as was his speech.

But when sober, the duke continued to behave as a duke. She hoped he was still feeling the effects of the liquor, for his expression was most forbidding, and she hoped it was not she that had put the look of disgust on his face. Or, worse yet, that his foul mood was habitual. Perhaps it was only the strain of travel, for they had been almost two full days on the road.

For whatever reason, her new husband sat rigidly in his seat across from her, showing no desire to close the distance between them.

And in response, she felt repelled from him.

It was foolish to care on that account. Jem's original fears were quite the contrary to the truth. He had imagined her wrestling a brute for her virtue in the back of a moving carriage. But this man no more desired the physical contact of his spouse than she did herself.

The chatty voyage to Gretna had been replaced with an uninterested silence that she suspected could stretch the length of the trip and far into the future.

And it was all right with her, she reminded herself. Once they were settled, she would return to her books and would appreciate a husband who was not likely to interrupt her work with demands for her attention.

Still, there were things that must be decided before they arrived in London. And that would be impossible without some communication.

She cleared her throat, hesitating to speak.

He looked up at her expectantly.

'I was wondering if you had considered what we might do once we reach London.'

'Do?'

'Well, yes. I wish to go to my bank, of course. And make my father's solicitors aware of my change in status.'

He nodded.

'But once that is done? Well, we cannot very well

live with my brother. There is room, of course, but I doubt that it would be in any way comfortable…'

He was staring at her and she fell into embarrassed silence. He spoke. 'When we arrive in the city, we will be going directly to my townhouse, and can make the financial arrangements after that.'

'Your townhouse.'

'Of course.'

She readied an objection, but paused before speaking. He was her husband, after all. And a man used to being obeyed. Insisting on her own way in this was liable to meet with objections. She said, 'Wherever we reside, I will need room for my collection of books, which is quite substantial. And a quiet place to study. A London townhouse might not be the best choice…'

He sighed, quite out of patience with her. 'Perhaps not the ones you have seen. But I assure you, the Bellston property in London is more than sufficient. We will not be staying there for long, since no one of any fashion is in London at this time. We will adjourn to the manor, once you have settled your business.'

'Manor?'

He was still looking at her as though she were an idiot. 'My home. I have a hunting lodge near Scotland, as well. I was visiting there when you found me. But there is no reason for you to see it at this time or ever, if you have no interest.'

'A manor,' she repeated.

His expression had grown somewhat bemused. 'And where did you think I lived, madam? Under a bridge?'

'I did not think on it. At all.' And now she looked

foolish. It annoyed her even more that she probably was. She had acted in a fit of temper, without considering the consequences.

'So you truly gave no thought to my title.' There was still a touch of amazement in the statement, as though he found the fact hard to comprehend, even after two days' trying. 'The peerage has both responsibilities as well as advantages. A title such as mine comes with a reward of land. In many years, it is a gift, but in some, it is a burden. In either case, I cannot simply walk away from it to indulge a whim.'

'A burden?'

'A recent fire has left portions of the manor house unlivable. Repairs are in effect, even as we speak. Expensive repairs,' he added significantly.

She nodded, understanding his most specific request for funds.

'Most of the house is livable, but I have business to complete in town. And so we will remain for a time in London, and reside in the townhouse. You will find space ample for your needs, I assure you.'

'That is good to know.' She was not at all sure that it was, but there was little she could do to change it.

'We will go to your bank as soon as you wish. You will introduce me as your new husband, and I shall need to make it clear to my solicitors that I have taken a wife. I doubt we can escape without the marriage becoming an *on dit,* for it is rather irregular.'

And there was another thing to worry about. She had not taken into account that his social life would be disrupted by the sudden marriage. No wonder he seemed cross. For her part, the idea was more than a little disturbing.

He continued. 'As soon as is possible, we shall retire to the country. We will take your books, of course. Have no fear of that. I doubt anyone shall wonder very much about us, once we are out of the public eye. I will need to return for Parliament, next session. But whether you choose to accompany me is your own affair.'

She searched his plan for flaws and found none. After the initial shock of it wore off, of course. She had expected to choose her own dwelling, and that her circumstances might diminish after leaving her brother's home. Why did she need a large house when a smaller one would suit her needs? But a manor…

'Did you have a better solution?' There was a touch of acid in the tone, but it was said mildly enough, considering.

He had taken pains to assure her that she would not lose her books. The least she could do was attempt to be co-operative. 'No. No. That is most satisfactory.'

'Satisfactory.' His mouth quirked. 'My holdings are not so rich as some, but I assure you that you will find them much more than satisfactory, once the improvements have been made.'

'Of course.'

Silence fell again. She looked down at her hands and out at the passing countryside, trying to appear comfortable. So, she was to be lady of a manor in the country. What part of the country? She had forgotten to ask. It would make her appear even more ignorant, if she waited until they were packed and driving toward it, to inquire.

Of course, once she was back in London, it would be easy enough to find the information, without having to ask her husband.

Unless her failure to ask made her appear uninterested in her new spouse...

It was all becoming very confusing.

He cleared his throat. 'This brother of yours. Is he a printer as well?' There was a pause. 'Because the servant mentioned that your father had been. And I thought, perhaps, family business...' He trailed off, displaying none of the eloquence that she had expected from him. Apparently, he was as uncomfortable in his ignorance as she was with hers.

She smiled and looked back at him. 'Yes. It is a family business. My father loved it dearly, and the books as well. And reading them, of course. He and Mother named us from the classics. My brother's name is Hector. Father always said that education was a great equaliser.'

'It is fortunate that a lack of education does not work in the same way. I was sent down from Oxford. It has had little effect on my status.'

They fell silent, again. She longed to ask why he had been forced to leave Oxford, but did not wish to seem impertinent. Was he like her brother had been, unimpressed by her desire for scholarship?

If so, he was biding his time before making the fact known. He'd had ample opportunity in the last few days to point out her foolishness over the translation. But he had said nothing yet.

'Marriage is also a great equaliser,' he said, to no one in particular.

Did he mean to refer to her sudden rise in society? If so, it was most unfair of him. She looked at him sharply. 'Apparently so. For once we reach the bank, your fortune shall be the equal of mine.'

She noted the flash of surprise in his eyes, as though she had struck him. And she waited with some trepidation for the response.

Then his face cleared, and he laughed. And suddenly she was sharing the carriage with the man she thought she had married. '*Touché*. I expect I will hear similar sentiments once my friends get wind of our happy union, but I had not expected to hear them from my own wife. I recommend, madam, that you save some of that sharp tongue to respond to those that wish to offer you false compliments on your most fortunate marriage.'

People would talk.

Well, of course they would. Why had she not realised the fact? And they would talk in a way that they never would have had she married the drunken nobody she was seeking. She was a duchess.

She would be noticed. And people would laugh.

A hand touched her, and she jumped, and realised that she had forgotten she was not alone in the carriage. She looked up into the face of her new husband, and read the concern on his face.

'Are you all right?' He said it very deliberately, as though he expected her to misunderstand. 'For a moment, you looked quite ill.'

'It is nothing. We have been travelling for some time, and the trip…' She let her words drift away, allowing him to make what he would of them.

'Shall I tell the driver to stop?'

'No, really. I will be fine.'

'Perhaps if we switch seats—a change of direction might help.' He took her hands and pulled her up off her bench, rising and pivoting gracefully in the tight space of the rocking carriage, to take her place and give her his. Then he pulled the shade on the window so that the moving scenery did not addle her gaze.

'Thank you.' She did still feel somewhat faint at the realisation of what she had done by marrying, and the impact it might have on the rest of her life. The distant and strange idea occurred to her that her husband was being most helpful and understanding about the whole thing. And that it might be nice to sit beside him, and rest her head against his shoulder for a time, until the world stopped spinning around her.

Which was a ludicrous idea. He was solicitous, but he had done nothing to make her think she was welcome to climb into his coat pocket. She looked at him again, even more beautiful in his concern for her, and closed her eyes against the realisation that they were a ridiculous study in contrast. A casual observer could not help but comment on it.

If he noticed the clamminess of her hand, which he still held, he did not comment, but reached out with his other hand as well, to rub some warmth back into the fingers. 'We will be in the city soon. You will feel much better, I am sure, once we have had some refreshment and a change of clothes.'

She certainly hoped so, for she doubted that she could feel any worse.

Chapter Five

When she opened her eyes a while later, the carriage was pulling up in front of a row of fine houses, and he tapped on the door, waiting for the servants to open it and put down the step. Then he descended and offered his hand to her. 'My dear?'

She reached out nervously to take it, while her mind raced to argue that she was in no way dear to him. The endearment was both inaccurate and unnecessary.

He saw the look in her eyes, and said, before she could speak, 'It might go easier with the servants if we maintain a pretence of familiarity. They will obey you, in any case. They would be foolish not to. But all the same…'

She nodded. 'Thank you, Adam.' There. She had said his name.

A footman opened the door before them, and she entered on the arm of the duke, who greeted the butler with a curt, 'Assemble the staff. Immediately.'

The man disappeared. He reappeared a short time later, accompanied by what Penny assumed must be the cook and the housekeeper, and, as she watched, an assortment of maids and footmen appeared from various entrances, lining up in an orderly row behind them.

She counted them. It must be a great house, as he had said, to need a staff so large. The home she had managed for her brother had made do with a staff of four. She reminded herself with some firmness that they were only servants and it did not do to show her fear of them.

The duke looked out over the small crowd assembled. 'I have called you all out from below stairs for an announcement. On my recent trip north, things did not go quite as expected.' He paused. 'Actually, they went much better than I expected. I married.'

There was an audible gasp from the room, before the servants managed to regain control of their emotions.

'May I present her Grace, the Duchess of Bellston—'

Before she could stop herself, she felt her knees begin to curtsy to the non-existent duchess, and her husband's hand came out to lift her back to her feet.

'—formerly, Miss Penelope Winthorpe. In celebration of this fact, you may all take the rest of the day off, to do as you will.'

There was an unexpected moment of tension.

'With pay, of course,' he added, and she could feel the staff relax again. 'We will be dining out. You need do nothing on our behalf until breakfast.'

The gasp had turned to a murmur of excitement, as the staff realised their good fortune.

'Three cheers for his Grace and the new lady of the

house.' The butler made an offer of 'huzzah' sound subdued and polite, but she accepted it with pleasure, as did her husband. 'Thank you. And now, you are dismissed. Enjoy the rest of your day.'

As quickly as they had gathered, the staff evaporated.

She looked at him, waiting for some indication of what was to be done next.

He glanced around him, seeking inspiration. 'Perhaps, a tour of the rooms would be in order. And then we will refresh ourselves, before a trip to your bankers.'

She nodded. 'An excellent plan. Please, your Grace, lead the way.'

He flinched. 'Remember, I am to be Adam to you. And you shall be?' He cocked his head to the side. 'Do you prefer Penelope, or are you a Penny?'

'Penny.'

'Then Penny it shall be, and whatever small endearments I can muster. Come, Penny.' There was a hesitation, as though he was struggling with a foreign language. 'Let me show you your home in London.' He led her down a short corridor, to doors that led to a parlour, which was grand; and a dining room, grander still, with room to seat twenty people. At the back of the house were a study, and a morning room.

'And this shall be yours.' He gestured into the sitting room, hesitating in the doorway as though he were afraid to enter.

She could understand why. Whoever had decorated the room had been the most ladylike of ladies. The furniture was gilt and satin, with legs so delicately turned that she was almost afraid to sit on it. If she chose a second sandwich at tea, the settee might collapse from the additional weight. And the desk, which would need to hold her books and writing materials, looked as though it might faint dead away, if expected to hold anything more serious than social correspondence. The other tables in the room were too small for anything larger than a rosebud, which would have to be candy pink to match the horrible silk upon the walls. The total was so sweet it made her teeth ache to look at it.

She looked in disgust at the ormolu clock on the mantel, which was supported by tiny gold goats and overflown with cherubs.

In response to her glare, the clock chimed the quarter hour, if such a stubbornly unobtrusive bell could be considered a chime.

She looked to her husband and struggled to speak. The correct response should have been 'thank you'. But it was quite beyond her. Eventually she said, 'It is very—pretty.'

He nodded in apology. 'We can find you furniture more suitable for work, and install additional shelves.' He pointed to a rather foolish collection of porcelain shepherds that graced a corner of the room. 'The bric-a-brac and nonsense can be dispensed with, if you wish.'

She looked dubiously around her.

'The room itself is large enough, is it not?'

She tried to ignore the design, and focus on the dimensions. It was larger than the one she had been using. She nodded.

'Very good, then. Redo it to suit yourself. I expected nothing less than that, from whatever woman I married. The rest of the house as well. If you see something that does not suit your tastes, it is well in your power to change it.' He paused. 'Except for my rooms, if you please. I would prefer that my bedroom and study remain as they are now.'

'I think that is not an issue. For I have seen nothing so far that needs alteration, and have no desire to change everything for change's sake.' She neglected to point out that, since any cosmetic changes to the house were to be made with her money, it hardly seemed like a sensible use of the funds. 'But this—' she gestured into her new work room '—must go.'

'Thank you.' He seemed relieved as well. There had a been tension in his back that eased as she said the words, and she suspected the first marital hurdle had been jumped with ease. He made no effort to open the door to his study, and she suspected that he wished some areas of his life to remain unviewed as well as untouched.

Fair enough.

'Let us go upstairs, then, and see the bedrooms.' He led her up the wide marble staircase and turned to the left, opening a door for her. 'These will be your rooms. There is a bedroom, a dressing room and a small room for your maid.'

None of which had been aired, she noted. The fire-place was cold and empty, and there was an uncomfortable chill in the unused room.

He noticed it as well, and wrinkled his nose. 'Well. Hmm. It seems I spoke too soon, when sending the staff away for a day of celebration. I have left no one to light you a fire.' He stepped across the room and opened a connecting door to his suite. There was a nervous pause. 'And I see the servants have brought your things to my room. They assumed…' He looked back at her, helplessly. 'This is not as it appears.'

What upset him more? she wondered—that she might think he wished to bed her, or that the servants had assumed that he would? 'It is all right. We will work things out between us, somehow.'

He nodded. 'Do you wish to change? You are welcome to use my room. There is a basin of fresh water. And clean towels. I could send for a maid to help you… Oh, damn. If you need help, I suppose, I…'

She imagined the feel of his hands at her back, undoing buttons. 'No. Thank you. I have become most adept at managing for myself, if there is no one to help me. If you will give me but a few minutes?'

He nodded and stepped aside, allowing her access to his room.

As the door shut behind her, she went hurriedly to the portmanteau on the floor and chose a fresh gown, struggling briefly with the closures at her back and slipping out of the travelling dress. Then she splashed some water from the basin on to her face, slipped into the new gown and used her brush to arrange her hair as best as was possible.

She could not help it, but glanced in the mirror behind her, examining the room. The man they had rescued from the street was obviously wealthy, but had seemed to have little care for health, his own cleanliness or welfare.

But the room behind her was orderly and immaculate. A sign of good housekeeping, perhaps. But there was more to it than that. The items in the room were expensive but well used and well cared for. The style and arrangement were elegant but simple. The whole suggested a well-ordered mind in repose. It gave her some level of comfort, knowing that her new husband's private rooms looked as they did. This was what she had expected from the Duke of Bellston.

She opened the door to the wardrobe and examined the line of coats and neatly hung breeches and trousers, and the row of brightly polished boots. Expensive, but not gaudy. The man was well tailored, but not a dandy. If he had sunk his fortune because he was prone to excess, there was no indication of it here.

From behind her, he cleared his throat.

She whirled, shutting the wardrobe door behind her.

'I am sorry. I knocked, but obviously you did not hear. Is there something you needed?'

That would cause her to snoop in his closet? He did not finish the sentence, allowing her a scrap of pride to hide her embarrassment. 'No. I am quite finished, thank you.'

'Then I would like to use my room as well, if you do not mind…' There was a hint of challenge there, but his face showed bland inquiry.

'I'll just wait downstairs. In the sitting room?'

'Thank you.'

She turned and exited the room before he could see the blush on her cheek, retracing her steps to her room on the first floor.

Adam waited for the click of the door latch before struggling out of his coat. It would be easier to call for his valet and admit that he had spoken in haste when releasing the staff. But he could manage to do for himself, if his wife had done so. And a day of leisure for the servants would unite them in support of the new mistress, and quell fears of upheaval and negative gossip. The minor inconvenience would be worth the gains in goodwill. He untied his cravat and tossed it aside, washing his face in the basin. Then he chose fresh linen, managing a sloppy knot that he hoped looked more Byronic than inept. He glanced behind him at the open door of the wardrobe.

She'd been searching his room. The thought should have annoyed him, but instead it made him smile. His new bride had a more-than-healthy curiosity. He walked over and pulled a coat off its hanger to replace his travelling clothes. Then she'd likely have been disappointed. There was nothing to see here. No skeletons. And not, fortunately, the bodies of any previous wives. Perhaps he should reassure her, lest she think him some sort of Bluebeard.

He glanced at her portmanteau on the floor beside the bed. Two could play at that game. Although what he expected to find, he was not sure.

He laid his hand on a spare gown, a clean chemise, a night rail, trimmed with embroidery and lace. It was all to be expected. Neatly folded and cared for, even though his wife travelled without a maidservant. The case was large and very heavy for only a few days' travel. But that was very like a woman, was it not? To pack more than was absolutely necessary. His hand stopped short of the bottom of the bag.

Books. Homer. Ovid. A book of poetry, with a ribbon tucked between the pages so that the reader would not lose her place. Not the readings of a mind given to foolish fancy.

He replaced things carefully, the way he had found them, and turned to go to meet her in the sitting room. She was as studious as she claimed, if she could not manage a few days without some sort of reading material. And it was well that she had brought her own to his house. There were many books he fully intended to read, when he had leisure. But for the life of him, he could not think what they would be, and he certainly did not have anything to read in the London house that held any enjoyment. It probably made him look a bit odd, to be without a library but well stocked in Meissen shepherds. But there was little he could do to change that now.

He approached her room in trepidation. The door was closed. Should he knock or enter freely? It was one of many decisions they would have to make together. If they did not mean to live as most married couples, then boundaries of privacy would have to be strictly observed.

At last, he settled on doing both: he knocked and then opened the door, announcing himself and thinking it damn odd that he should need to do it in his own house.

His wife looked up from a book.

'You have found something to read?' he said, and wished he did not sound so surprised at the fact.

'There were a stack of books on the shelf, here. Minerva novels. And Anne Radcliff, of course.' She glanced around her. 'Overblown and romanticised. They are most suited to the décor.'

'They are not mine,' he said, alarmed that such things even existed on the premises.

'That is a great comfort. For I would wish to rethink our bargain were they yours.' There was a twinkle in her eye as she said it. 'But if you favour melodrama, I suspect that this afternoon's meetings will be quite entertaining.'

And she was correct in what she said, for the trip to his wife's bank was most diverting. He was not familiar with the location, which was far from Bond Street, nor did the men working there know him. But it was obvious that they knew his wife and held her in respect. She was ushered into a private office before she even needed to speak her request.

When her bankers entered the room, she wasted no time on introductions, but straight away announced that she had married, and that all business matters must be turned over, post haste, to her new husband.

He could not help but enjoy the look of shock on the faces of the bankers. There was a moment of stunned silence, before the men sought to resist, arguing that the union had been most impulsive and possibly unwise. They eyed him suspiciously, and hinted at the danger of fortune hunters where such a large sum was involved. Was she sure that she was making the correct decision? Had she consulted her brother in the matter?

Adam watched as his new wife grew very still, listening in what appeared to be respectful silence. Although there were no outward signs, he suspected the look of patience she radiated was a sham. And at last, when they enquired if she had obtained her brother's permission to wed, her cool exterior evaporated.

'Gentlemen, I am of age, and would not have needed my brother's permission if the decision to take a husband had taken a year instead of a day. In any case, it is too late now, for I cannot very well send the man away, explaining that our marriage was just a passing fancy on my part. Nor do I wish to.

'May I introduce my husband, and manager of all my finances from here on, Adam Felkirk, Duke of Bellston.'

He did his best to maintain an unaffected visage, although the desire was strong to laugh aloud at the sight of the two men, near to apoplexy, bowing and calling him 'your Grace', and offering tea, whisky or anything he might desire, hoping to erase the words 'fortune hunter' from the previous conversation.

'No, thank you. I merely wish to see the account book that holds the recent transactions on my wife's inheritance.'

The men looked terrified now, but the account book appeared, along with a cup of tea.

Adam glanced down the row of figures, shock mingling with relief. His financial problems were solved, for there was more than enough to effect repairs on the house, and tide the property over until a more favourable season. He was equally glad that he had known nothing of the numbers involved when he had wed the girl. Considering his financial condition, he feared he'd have lost all shame, fallen at her feet, and begged her to wed him, based on what he saw before him.

He looked at the line of monthly withdrawals, increasing in amount as time passed. 'Do you have any regular expenses that need to be met, my dear?'

'Not really. My brother allows me a small allowance, and I take care not to exceed it. I doubt I'll need more than twenty or thirty pounds a month.'

Which was far less than the expenditures on the account. He tapped the paper with his fingertip and glanced up at the bankers. Where was the money going? To the only man with access to the account.

Until now, that is.

Hector had not touched the principal, as of yet. But Penny had been correct in her fears. If measures were not taken, there would be no fortune left to hunt.

He smiled, as condescending and patronising as he could manage. 'You gentlemen were wise to be concerned with the prudence of my wife's decision. But you need concern yourself no longer. Please prepare a draft, in this amount...' he scribbled a number in the book '...and send it to my bankers. I will give you the direction. The rest can remain here, as long as the investments continue to be as profitable as they have been. But under no circumstances is anyone to have access to the account other than myself.' He glanced at Penelope. 'Or my wife, of course. She has my permission to do as she pleases in the matter. Should she send any bills to you, please honour them immediately.'

He shot a sidelong glance at Penelope, and watched her eyes go bright and her mouth make a tiny 'O' of surprise.

He smiled. 'Is that to your satisfaction, dear?'

'Very much so.' The smile on her face was softer than it had been, with none of the hesitance that he had seen in her from the first day. Her body relaxed enough so that her arm brushed the sleeve of his jacket.

She trusted him. At least, for now.

And it cleared the doubts in his own heart, that he had married her for her money. Her fortune could stay separate from his, and he would leave her the control of it. With the look she was giving him, he felt almost heroic.

He was quite enjoying it.

After the success at the bankers, Penny had hoped to feel more confidence when confronting her brother. But as she entered the house, she could feel all the old fears reforming in her. Living here had felt a prison, as much as a haven. And her brother's continual reminders that this was all she would ever know, since no one would want her, had reinforced the iron bars around her.

And now, after only a few days away, the house felt strange. It was as though she were visiting a friend and not returning to her home. She had not realised how thoroughly she had put it behind her, once she made her decision. But it was comforting to think that there would be no foolish longing for the past, now that she was settling into her new life. Once she had her clothing and her things, there was no reason to return again.

She rang for servants, signifying that a maid should be sent to her room to pack her belongings, and sent Jem and another footman to the library with instructions for the crating and removal of her books and papers.

In the midst of her orders, her brother hurried into

the room and seized her by the arm. 'Penny! You have returned, at last. When I realised that you were gone I was near frantic. Do you not realise the risk to your reputation by travelling alone? Especially when you gave me no indication of where you were going. I absolutely forbid such actions in the future. I cannot believe…' Hector appeared ready to continue in his speech without ceasing, and showed no indication that he had recognised the presence of another in the room.

It annoyed her to think that he cared more about her disobedience than he did her safety. She pulled away from him, and turned to gesture to the man in the corner. 'Hector, may I present my husband, the Duke of Bellston. Adam, this is my brother, Hector.' She hoped she had not hesitated too much on the word Adam. She did not wish to appear unfamiliar with the name.

Hector ran out of air, mid-sentence, taking in a great gasp before managing, 'Husband?'

'Yes,' she replied as mildly as possible. 'When last we spoke, I indicated to you that I intended to marry, to settle the question of who should control my inheritance. And so I have married.'

'But you cannot.'

'Of course I can. I am of age, after all.'

'You cannot expect me to take a stranger into our home, on the basis of such a brief introduction.'

Her husband stood the rebuke mildly.

'Of course I do not. I have come for my possessions and will be moving them to my new home as soon as is possible.'

'Your new home.' Apparently, her brother was having some problem following the speed of events.

'Yes, Hector. I will be living with my husband, now that I am married.'

'You will do nothing of the kind. I have had more than enough of your nonsense. This is what comes of too much learning. Ideas. And telling jokes that are in no way funny. You will go to your room, and I will apologise to this gentleman, whoever he may be. And tomorrow, we will all go to the solicitors and straighten out the mess you have created.'

This time, she did not even bother to count. 'I will go to my room, Hector. To gather my clothing. From there, I mean to go to the library and the study, and empty them as well. And then I will be gone from this house and your presence. You have no power over me to stop it. And that, Hector, is what comes of not enough reading.'

His face was growing red, and he was readying a response.

And from behind her, she heard her husband, quietly clearing his throat. His voice was mildness and reason itself. 'Perhaps, Penny, it would be best if you saw to your packing, while I speak to your brother.'

She had the most curious feeling that he had issued a command, although it showed in neither his face nor his voice.

She opened her mouth to object, and then remembered how effectively he had dealt with the bankers. If he wished her to leave the room, then perhaps there was a reason for it. It would serve no purpose, challenging him in front of her brother. That would only prove Hector's point: that she had been foolish to marry in the first place. She blinked at Adam for a moment, then shrugged her shoulders and said, 'Very well.' And then she left the room, shutting the doors almost completely behind her.

Then she turned back and put her ear to the crack.

Her husband waited for a moment, giving her enough time to get to her room, she suspected. And then he waited even longer.

When the silence became oppressive, Hector blurted, 'Now see here, sir—'

Adam responded, 'The correct form of address when speaking to me is "your Grace". Perhaps you did not know it, since you obviously have little acquaintance with the peerage. But since we are family now...' disdain dripped from the last words '...you may call me Adam.'

Hector snorted. 'You cannot expect me to believe that Penny has been gone from the house less than a week, and has returned not only a married woman, but a duchess.'

Adam said, 'Your belief is not a requirement, Mr Winthorpe. The marriage exists. The bankers have been informed of it, and I have taken control of my wife's inheritance.'

This last seemed to give her brother pause, for he took a moment before letting out a weak laugh. 'But you cannot wish to be married to my sister. She is a nothing. A nobody.' There was another pause, and his tone changed. 'Albeit, a very wealthy nobody. And that could not possibly have influenced your decision when seeking such a humble bride—'

'Stop right there.' Adam did not shout, but the command in the tone was no longer an implication. 'I recommend that you pause to think before speaking further.' His voice dropped to just above a whisper. 'Here are the facts, and you would do well to remember them. Penelope is neither a nothing, nor a nobody. She is her Grace, the Duchess of Bellston. It will do you no good to hint that I am after her fortune, since she has gained as much, if not more, than I have by the union.'

There was another long pause, to allow the facts to sink into the thick skull of her brother. And then Adam said, 'But you have lost by her marriage, have you not? I've seen the books at the bank, and the withdrawals you have been making to keep your business afloat.'

Hector sputtered, 'I've done nothing of the kind. Those monies were for Penelope's expenses.'

'Then it shall not matter to you in the least that I am willing to take the management of the monies out of your hands. I can take care of my wife's bills without your help. You need trouble yourself no further with the management of her funds, but devote the whole of your time to business.' Her husband's tone clearly said, 'Dismissed.'

Penny covered her mouth to stifle a laugh.

But her brother refused to yield all. His voice rose to near a shout. 'All right, then. Very well. She has married and you have taken her money, and her as well. I wish you luck, your Grace, for you will find her fractious nature, her impulsive temper and her unending stubbornness to be more curse than blessing. She may pack her clothes and leave immediately, if she is so eager to do it. But she shall leave the books where they are. I have no intention of allowing her to put the contents of the family library into trunks and carry them from the house.'

Her husband seemed to consider on it, and then replied, with a neutral, 'If she wishes it, then it shall be so.'

Her brother shouted back, 'But it will leave the shelves empty!'

Adam responded quietly, 'That should not present much of a problem. You are a book printer, are you not? Bring home something from work to fill the shelves. I doubt it matters much what the titles may be, if one has no intention of reading them.'

If her brother recognised the insult to his intelligence, he let it pass without comment. 'This has nothing to do with whether I wish to read the books in question.'

'I thought not.'

'It is the value of the things. Do you know how many pounds has been spent to furnish that room?'

'Quite a few, I should think. She purchased many of those books herself, did she not?'

'When I could not manage to stop her.'

Adam's voice was cool reason. 'Then I see no reason that she need purchase them twice to stock the library in her new home. It is not as if she will be returning here to study.'

And still her brother would not give up. 'See here, you. You cannot think to take her from her family.'

'That is generally what happens when one marries,' Adam said, in a bored drawl. 'There is something in the

Bible about it, although I cannot say I remember the words. She is cleaving unto me, now. You have nothing to say in the matter of her future.'

Penny could almost imagine the wave of his hand, as he dismissed her brother's argument.

'Only because you have stolen her from me,' Hector snapped.

'Stolen her?' The duke laughed out loud. 'How long have you known your sister, sir? Is there some chance that you are adopted, or that she is some changeling, recently added to your family? I have limited acquaintance with her, I'll admit. But in that time I have learned enough to know that it would be exceptionally difficult to steal her from a place she wished to be, or to dissuade her from a path she had chosen for herself.'

'But that does not mean that I will allow her to behave foolishly.'

She was angry before she could even remember to count, and grabbed the door handle, ready to push her way back into the room and tell her brother that, after all that had been said and done, he had no right on earth to control her.

But Adam cut in before she could move. 'You have no authority over my wife. Penelope shall arrange for the transport of the library and the rest of her things to my townhouse. She shall do so at her own pace and in her own way. If I hear of any interference from you in the matter, if you place even the slightest obstruction in her way, I will take whatever action is necessary to thwart you, and it shall be my goal, henceforth, to see that you regret the impertinence. Are we in agreement?'

His voice held a cold fury that she had never heard before, and he was every bit the man she had imagined from *The Times*, so powerful that he could move the country with a few words.

Hector appeared to have been struck dumb, and so Adam answered for him. 'Very good. Our interview is at an end. I will be waiting in the carriage, should Penelope need me for anything. Which, for your sake, Mr Winthorpe, I sincerely hope she does not.'

Which meant he would be coming out into the hall in a moment, and he would realise that she was so lost to all manners as to listen at keyholes on private conversations. And, even worse, he might see the effect his speech had upon her, for her heart was fluttering so that she could hardly breathe.

She turned and sprinted towards the library, ducking into the open door, only to collide with Jem, knocking a case of books from his arms. The sound of the crash mingled with his bark of objection at people charging around the house and not watching where they were going.

Which in no way covered the faint chuckle she heard from the hall as her husband passed by on his way to the exit.

Chapter Six

Her heart was lighter, now that she had faced her brother at last. But empty as well. Hector was furious, and she'd cut herself off from the only home she'd ever known. It would have happened eventually, she supposed. Just as it should have happened four years before. But she had been prepared then. Now, the sudden marriage and all that came with it made her feel more alone than she had been, even though she had a life's companion to share it with.

And what a strange companion she had chosen. It had been much fun to watch him in action against her adversaries. And she hoped that her current feelings for him were not too apparent, for the afternoon's appointments and the masterful way he had handled things had left her breathless and not quite herself. She had half a mind to throw herself upon him, in a display of affection that would be most inappropriate towards a man who was nearly a stranger to her. And she feared that, if she spoke, she was liable to ramble on and sound as foolish as a schoolroom miss.

Her husband was seated opposite her in the hired carriage with a faint smile on his face, showing no effects of the day's changes. When she said nothing, he spoke. 'We have done a good day's work, I think. Your money is taken care of. Your things will be brought to the house tomorrow. I recommend that we send your manservant on his way, and attend to our supper, for we have missed tea, and I am feeling quite hungry. I can recommend several restaurants…'

Eating in public. She had always found it difficult to relax when in a crowd, and sitting down to a meal surrounded by strangers seemed to amplify those feelings. Suppose she were to order the wrong thing, use the wrong utensil when eating or break some other rule that would make her appear gauche to the duke or the people around them? If she took a simple meal in her rooms at the townhouse, she need have no worries of mistake. She would beg off, and save her husband the embarrassment of being seen with her. She said, 'I am accustomed to eat at home of an evening.'

'And I am not,' he said, with finality. 'I belong to several clubs— Boodle's, White's, Brooks's—and frequent them most evenings when I am in town. Of course, I cannot very well take you there. No ladies.' He stopped to consider his options.

So many clubs. It gave her a good idea where his wealth might have run to. And why he had needed so much of hers. 'It is more economical to dine at home,' she offered.

He raised an eyebrow and said, 'I imagine it is on such nights as the servants are engaged. My kitchen is most fine. You will know that soon enough. But remember, I have released the staff for the evening. You may go back, if you wish, and explain to them that economy requires they return to work.'

She gave a small shake of her head.

'I thought not. In the future, you may dine at home, as you wish. But do not be terribly surprised if I do not join you there, for I prefer society to peace and quiet. And tonight, we will dine out to celebrate the nuptials. That is only natural, is it not?'

She nodded hesitantly.

'I thought you would agree.' He smiled again, knowing that he was once more without opposition and gave directions to the driver.

On entering the restaurant, they were led by the head waiter to a prominent spot with the faintest murmur of 'your Grace'. Penny was conscious of the eyes of the strangers around them, tracking them to their table.

Her husband's head dipped in her direction. 'They are wondering who you are.'

'Oh, no.' She could feel the blood draining from her face and a lightness in her head as the weight of all the eyes settled upon her.

'My dear, you look quite faint.' He seemed genuinely concerned. 'Wine will restore you. And food and rest.' He signalled the waiter. 'Champagne, please. And a dinner fit for celebration. But nothing too heavy.' When his glass was filled, he raised it in toast to her. 'To my bride.'

The waiter took in the faintest breath of surprise, as did a woman at a nearby table, who had overheard the remark.

'Shh,' Penny cautioned. 'People are taking notice.'

'Let them,' Adam said, taking a sip. 'While you packed, I arranged for an announcement in tomorrow's *Times*. It is not as if it is to be a secret.'

'I never thought…'

'That you would tell anyone besides the bank that you had wed?'

'That anyone would care,' she said.

'I have no idea what people might think of your marriage,' he responded. 'But if I marry, all of London will care.'

She took a gulp of her own wine. 'That is most conceited of you, sir.'

'But no less true.'

'But there must be a better way to make the world aware than sitting in the middle of a public place and allowing the world to gawk at us,' she whispered.

He smiled. 'I am sorry. Have I done something to shame you, Penelope?'

'Of course not. We barely know—'

He cut her off before she could finish the sentence. 'Are you embarrassed to be seen with me?'

'Don't be ridiculous. You are the Duke of Bellston. Why would I be embarrassed?'

'Then I fail to understand why we should not be seen dining together, in a public place. It is not as if I do not wish my wife at my side.'

She was readying the argument that, of course, he

would not wish to dine with her. He was a duke, and she was a nobody. And he was every bit as beautiful as she was plain. And if he meant to embarrass her by showing the world the fact…

And then she looked at the way he was smiling at her. It was a kind smile, not full of passion, but containing no malice. And she imagined what it would be like, if he had dropped her at the townhouse, and gone on his merry way. Perhaps he would mention casually to some man at a club that he had wed. And there would be a small announcement in the papers.

People would wonder. And then, someone would see her, and nod, and whisper to others that it was obvious why the duke chose to leave his wife alone. When the most attractive feature was a woman's purse, you hardly need bring her along to enjoy the benefit.

Or, they could be seen in public for a time, and people might remark on the difference between them. But they would not think that the eventual separation of the two was a sign that he had packed her off to the country out of shame.

He watched as the knowledge came home to her. 'People will talk, Penny. No matter what we do. But there are ways to see that they speak aloud, and then lose interest. It is far less annoying, I assure you, than the continual whispering of those who are afraid to give voice to their suspicions.'

The plates arrived, and he offered her a bite of lobster on the end of his fork. 'Relax. Enjoy your dinner. And then we will go home.'

She took it obediently and chewed, numb with

shock. *Home. Together. With him.* The thoughts that flitted across her mind were madness. After the rough start in Scotland, her new husband was proving to be almost too perfect. In the space of a few hours, he had gained for her everything she could have wished. And now, if he would only let her go home and seclude herself in that horrible pink room before she said something foolish… If he insisted on staring at her as he had been with those marvellous blue eyes, and feeding her from his own plate as though she were a baby bird, who could blame her if she forgot that the need for familiarity was a sham, and began to think that deeper emotions were engaged.

There was a very subdued commotion at the entrance to the room, and Adam looked up. 'Aha. I knew news would travel quickly. But I had wondered how long it would take.'

A man strode rapidly toward them, weaving between the tables to where they sat. He noticed the space, set for two, and turned to the nearest empty table, seizing a chair and pulling it forward to them, seating himself between Penny and the duke. Then he looked at Adam and said, without preamble, 'When did you mean to inform me? Do you have any idea how embarrassing it is to be at one's club, enjoying a whisky and minding one's own business, only to have the man holding the book demanding that I pay my wagers on the date of your marriage? Of course I insisted that it was nonsense, for there was no way that such a thing would have occurred without my knowledge.'

Adam laughed. 'Ah, yes. I had forgotten the wagers.'

He looked sheepishly at Penny. 'I stand to lose a fair sum of money on that as well. I had bet against myself marrying within the year.'

Gambling, again. And losing. Another confirmation of her suspicions. 'You bet against yourself?'

He shrugged. 'I needed the money, and thought it must be a sure thing. But when I found you, darling, I quite forgot—'

'Darling?' the man next to her snapped. 'So it's true, then? You ran off to Scotland to get a wife, and told me nothing?'

'It did not occur to me until after,' Adam answered. 'Penny, may I present your brother-in-law, Lord William Felkirk. William, Penelope, my wife, the new duchess of Bellston.'

William stared at her, reached for his brother's wine glass and drained it.

William was a younger version of her husband. Not so handsome, perhaps, but he had a pleasant face, which would have been even more pleasant had it not been frozen in shock by the sight of her. Penny attempted a smile and murmured, 'How do you do?'

Will continued to stare at her in silence.

Adam smiled in her direction with enough warmth for both of them, and then looked back to his brother. 'Manners, Will. Say hello to the girl.'

'How do you do?' Will said without emotion.

'Penny is the heiress to a printer, here in London. We met when I was travelling.'

She could see the alarm in his eyes at the word printer, followed by a wariness. He examined her closely, and glanced from her to his brother. 'You were not long in the north, Adam. The trip lasted less than a week. Your marriage was most unexpected.'

'To us as well.'

He stared back at Penny, daring her to confirm the story. 'My brother never spoke of you.'

Her gaze dropped to her plate. 'We did not know each other for long before we married.'

'How fortunate for you to find a duke when you chose to wed. You must be enjoying your new title.' He had cut to the quick with no fuss.

'Frankly, I do not give it much thought.'

'Really.' He did not believe her.

Adam took a sip of wine. 'William, Penny's feelings on the matter of her sudden elevation to duchess are none of your concern. Now, join us in our celebration, for I wish you to be as happy as I am.' His voice held a veiled command.

Adam signalled for the waiter to bring another glass and plate, and they finished the meal in near silence, and William made no more attempts to question them.

Adam rubbed his temples and did his best to ignore the dull pain behind his eyes. It had been the longest meal of his life. First, he had needed to calm Penelope, who was clearly unaccustomed to the attention of the other diners. But he had done a fair job charming her back to good spirits. It had been going well, until Will had come and set things back on edge.

He'd had a good mind to tell his brother that the middle of a public dining room was no place to air the family laundry. If he could not manage to be a civil dinner companion, then he should take himself back to whatever foul cave he'd crawled from, and let them enjoy their food in peace.

When it was time to leave, William offered his carriage, and when they arrived at the townhouse, he followed them in, without invitation.

Adam should have refused him entrance, after his reprehensible behaviour in the restaurant. But if Will had anything to say on the subject of his brother's marriage, it might as well be said now and be over with, when the servants were away.

They were barely over the threshold before Will said, 'We must speak.' He glanced toward the study, then to Adam, totally ignoring the other person in the room.

Penny was aware of the slight. How could she not be, for Will made no effort to be subtle? She said, with false cheer, 'I will leave you two alone, then. Thank you for a most pleasant evening.'

Liar. But at least she was making an effort, which was more than he could say for his own family.

Penelope was barely clear of the room before William muttered, 'I will send for the solicitors immediately and we will put an end to this farce before anyone else learns of it.'

'The study, William,' he snapped, all patience gone.

They walked down the corridor, and he gestured Will into the room, slamming the door behind them.

Will paced the floor, not bothering to look in his direction. 'It has been only a few days, has it not? And most of that time, spent on the road. No one of importance has seen, I am sure. I will consult the lawyers, and begin the annulment proceedings. You will spend the night at your club, safely away from this woman.'

'I will do no such thing. I have no intention of leaving this house, and there will be no more talk of annulments.' Adam stalked past him, and threw himself into the chair behind the desk.

'You've lain with her already, have you?'

'That is none of your business, little brother.'

William nodded. 'I thought not. It is not a true marriage, but you have too much pride to admit the mistake.'

'This has nothing to do with pride.'

'Neither does it have to do with a sudden affection.'

Adam laughed. 'Affection? You expect me to marry for love, then?'

Will ceased his pacing and leaned over the desk, his fists planted on the wood. 'I think it is reasonable that there be at least a fondness between the two people involved. And it is plain that none exists between the two of you. You sat there at dinner with a false smile, pretending nothing was wrong, and she could barely look up from her plate.'

'We have an understanding.'

'That is rich.' Will snapped. 'She married you for your title, and you married her for her money. We can all claim the same understanding, for the fact is perfectly obvious to everyone who cares to look.'

'It is more complicated than that.'

'Do you mean to enlighten me as to how?'

Adam thought of the condition he'd been in when he'd made the decision to marry. And the condition just before, when he'd meant to end his life. 'No, I do not. That is something between my wife and myself.'

'Your wife.' Will snorted.

Adams hands tightened on the arms of his chair until he was sure that his fingers must leave marks in the wood. 'My wife, William. And I will thank you not to take that tone when referring to her. Despite what it may appear, I did not marry her for her money, any more than she sought to be a duchess. That we are both so blessed is a most fortunate occurrence, and I have no intention to annul. Lord knows, the estate needs the money she brings with her, and she has no objections to my using it.'

'So you will tie yourself to a woman that you do not love, just to keep the estate going.'

Adam stared at him, hardly understanding. 'Of course I would. If it meant that I could rebuild the house and protect the tenants until the next harvest time. Her money will mean the difference between success and failure this year.'

'What are the tenants to you, Adam? It is not as though they are family. And the manor is only a house.'

'It is my birthright,' Adam said. 'And I will do what is necessary to protect it. If it were you, would you not?'

William stared back at him, equally confused. 'I thank God every day that your title did not come to me. I have no desire to possess your lands, Adam.'

'But if it were to fall to you?' he pressed.

'Do not say that. For that would mean that you were dead. You are not ill, are you? Your line of questioning disturbs me.'

Adam waved his hand. 'No, no, I am not ill. It is only a rhetorical question. Do not read so much into it.'

'Then I will answer truthfully. No, I would not marry just for the sake of the title. Do not think you can marry for money to a woman you cannot bring yourself to bed, and then force me to be Bellston when you die without an heir. I would as soon see it all revert to the crown than become a slave to the land, as you are.'

Slavery? It was an honour. How could Will not understand? 'Search your heart and answer again. For it is quite possible that the whole thing will come to you, at any rate.'

Will waved the suggestion away. 'Not for long. If you mean to escape your responsibility with a hypothetical and untimely death, then two of us can play the game. I would rather die than inherit.'

Adam paused to thank God for the timely intervention of Penelope and her wild scheme. His death would have served no purpose if it had forced Will to take such action as he threatened. And he would not have wanted the heir he saw before him now. Will had always seemed so strong. Why had he never noticed that he was selfish as well?

Will continued. 'I suggest again that you seek an annulment if you do not wish for a legitimate heir from this poor woman. It is not fair to her, nor to me, for you to play with our fates in such a way, so that you can buy slate for your roof.'

Adam tried one last time. 'But if it falls to you…'

'I will take whatever measures are necessary to see that it does not.'

Damn it to hell. Here was another thing that he would have to contend with. Until now, he had assumed that there would be no problem with the succession. He had thought no further than the immediate crisis, just as he had thought no further when attempting suicide.

He must learn to play a longer game if he wished to succeed.

He looked to his brother again. 'I do not mean to abandon this life just yet, so you need not fear an inheritance. I had no idea that you felt so strongly about it.'

'I do.'

'Very well, then. No matter what may occur, you will not be the next duke. But neither do I intend to abandon my current plan just yet. The heir situation will sort itself out eventually, I suspect.'

'Do you, now?' His brother laughed. 'If you think it can sort itself out without some intervention on your part, then you are as cloth-headed as I've come to suspect. You wife is waiting in your bed, Adam. Let the sorting begin.'

Chapter Seven

Penny tried to put the mess downstairs behind her as she climbed the stairs to her room. William Felkirk had made little effort to disguise his distaste for her and was no doubt pouring poison in his brother's ears on the subject of marriage to upstart title hunters.

There was little she could do about it if Adam chose to listen. An acquaintance of several days and a trumped-up marriage were not equal to a bond of blood. She could only wait to see if he came to her room to explain that it had been a mistake, that he was terribly sorry, and that they would be undoing today's work in the morning.

She looked at her bedchamber and sighed, nearly overcome with exhaustion. No matter the outcome, she needed a warm bed and a good night's sleep. But the room in front of her was as cold and dark as it had been earlier in the day. If there was fuel available, she could manage to lay her own fire, but she could see by the light of her candle that the hearth and grate were empty. Not an ash remained.

She looked in trepidation at the connecting door to her husband's room. If she could borrow some coal and a Lucifer from his fire, and perhaps a little water from the basin, she could manage until the servants came back in the morning.

She knocked once; when there was no answer she pushed the door open and entered.

The bed had been turned down and a fire laid, despite the servants' day off. It was warm and cheerful, ready for occupation, and nothing like the room she had just left. There was a crystal bowl on the night table filled with red roses, and stray petals sprinkled the counterpane. Their fragrance scented the room.

Her portmanteau was nowhere to be seen, but her nightrail lay on the bed, spread out in welcome.

The door to the hall opened, and she looked back at her husband, leaning against the frame.

'My room is not prepared,' she said, to explain her presence.

He ran a hand through his hair in boyish embarrassment. 'The servants assume…'

She nodded.

He shrugged. 'You can hardly expect otherwise.'

'And what are we to do to correct the assumption?'

He stared at her. 'Why would we need to do that? That a man and a wife, newly married, might wish to share a bed is hardly cause for comment. But that a man and a woman, just wed, do not? That is most unusual. More gossip will arise from that than the other.'

She looked doubtful. 'I wondered if that might not matter to you so much now you have spoken to your brother.'

'Whatever do you mean?'

'That perhaps, now that you are back in your own home, you might wish to call a halt to our marriage. It is not too late, I think, to have second thoughts in the matter. And I would not fault you for it.'

'Because my brother does not approve?' He made no attempt to hide the truth from her. Although it hurt to hear it, his honesty was admirable.

He stepped into the room and closed the door behind him. 'What business is this of Will's? When he takes a wife, he will not wish me to trail along, giving offense and offering advice where none was requested. I recommend that you ignore Will as I intend to.' He moved across the room to a chair, sat down and set to work removing his boots.

Very well, then. There had been no change in her status. But what was to happen now? Did he mean to change in front of her? She was torn between embarrassment and a growing curiosity. How far did he mean to take their marriage? They had discussed nothing like this on the road from Scotland.

Then he stood up and walked across the room in his stockinged feet, locked the door and dragged the heavy comforter from the bed across the room to his chair. 'It shall not be the finest bed in London, but I have had worse.' He gestured to the rose-strewn mattress on the other side of the room. 'Be my guest.'

She sat on the edge of the bed and watched him as

he divested himself of coat and waistcoat, untied his cravat and undid his cuffs. He sat down again, slouching into the chair, long legs stretched out before him, wrapped the comforter around his body, and offered her a sketch of a salute, before closing his eyes.

She blew out her candle, placed her spectacles on the night table beside the bed, removed her slippers and stretched out on top of the sheets, arms folded over her chest.

From across the room, her husband's voice came as a low rumble. 'Is that how you mean to sleep? It cannot be comfortable.'

'For you either,' she said.

'But at least I am not fully dressed. Shall I call someone to help you out of your gown?'

'I can manage the gown myself, for I am most limber and can reach the hooks. But that would leave the corset, and I fear the lacing is too much for me. If we do not wish the servants to gossip, then I think not.'

He sighed and got out of his chair. 'I shall help you, then.'

'That would be most improper.'

He laughed. 'For better or worse, madam, I am your husband. It is the most proper thing in the world.'

She hesitated.

'It will look much stranger to have the maid undo the laces tomorrow than to let me do it tonight. Here, slide to the edge of the bed, and turn your back to me.'

She sat up and crawled to where he could reach her, turning her back to him. She could feel his touch, businesslike, undoing the hooks of the bodice and pushing it open wide until it drooped down her shoulders. She tensed.

'You needn't worry, you know. I will not hurt you or damage the gown.' He laughed softly. 'I have some small experience with these things. In fact, I can do it with my eyes closed if that makes you feel more comfortable.'

It would be ludicrous to describe the sensations she was experiencing as comfort. It would have been comforting to have the efficient, easily ignored hands of a maid to do the work. She would have climbed into bed and not thought twice about it.

But a man was undressing her. And since he had closed his eyes, it seemed he needed to work more slowly to do the job. He had placed his hand on her shoulders and squeezed the muscles there in his large palms before sliding slowly over the bare skin of her upper back and down the length of the corset to the knot at the bottom. He reached out to span her waist, and she drew a sharp breath as he undid the tie of her petticoat and pushed it out of the way. Then he leaned her forward slightly, and his fingers returned to the corset to work the knot free.

She could feel it loosen, and tried to assure him that she could manage the rest herself, but no breath would come to form the words.

He was moving slowly upwards, fingers beneath the corset, pulling the string free of the eyelets, one set at a time. She could feel the warmth of his hands through the fabric of her chemise, working their way up her body until the corset was completely open.

There was a pause that seemed like for ever as his hands rested on her body, only the thin cotton between his touch and her skin. And then he moved and the corset slipped free. She folded her arms tight to her chest, trying to maintain some modesty before it fell away to leave her nearly bare.

'Can you manage the rest?' His voice was annoyingly clear and untroubled.

She swallowed. 'I think so. Yes.'

'Very well, then. Goodnight, Penelope.'

And she heard him returning to his chair.

She squinted at him from across the room, until she was reasonably sure that his eyes were closed and he would see nothing. She hurried to remove her clothing, throwing it all to the floor and diving into her nightgown and under the sheets, safely out of sight.

She settled back on to the bed, pulling the linens up over her and waiting for sleep that did not come. The fire was dying, and the chill was seeping into the corners, though her skin still tingled with the heat from his touch.

It probably meant nothing to him. He was familiar with women's garments and the removing of them. He had done what he had done many times before, albeit with different results.

Her unwilling mind flashed to what it would have been like, if she was anyone other than who she was. His hands would be as slow and gentle as they had been while undoing her dress. Only, when the laces of the stays were undone, he would not stop touching her. Instead, he would lean forwards, and his lips would come down upon her skin.

She stared at the canopy of the bed, eyes wide, unable to stop the pictures playing in her mind and the phantom feeling of his hands and his mouth. Her body gave an uncontrollable shudder in response.

Across the room from her, her husband stirred in his chair, and rose, moving through the darkness towards her.

Without warning, the comforter dropped upon her body, and his hands smoothed it over her, tucking it close about her. Warmth flooded her, the warmth of his own body, left in the quilt. She sighed happily.

He returned to his chair, stretched out and slept.

Chapter Eight

When she awoke, light was seeping through the cracks in the bed curtains, which had been drawn at some point during the night. She could hear movement, and hushed voices from the other side. She sat up and placed her ear to the crack, so that she could listen.

Her husband. Talking to a servant, who must be his valet. Arranging for someone in the staff who would serve as a lady's maid, temporarily, at least. Perhaps permanently, since he was unsure if her Grace had servants of her own whom she wished to bring to the household. He had not discussed the matter with her.

The valet hurried away, and the door closed. She could hear her husband approaching the bed, and she pulled back from the curtain.

'Penny?' He said it softly, so as not to startle a sleeper.

'Yes?'

'May I open the curtains?'

'Yes.' Her voice was breathless with excitement, and she cleared her throat to cover the fact. As the light streamed in and hit her, she rubbed her eyes and yawned, trying to appear as though she had just awakened.

Adam was wrapped in a dressing gown, and she could see flashes of bare leg when she looked down. She must remember not to look down, then, for the thought that he was bare beneath his robe made her feel quite giddy.

'Did you sleep well?' He was solicitous.

'Very. Thank you. Your bed is very comfortable.' She glanced in the direction of the chair. 'I am sorry that you did not have the same luxury.'

Which might make it sound like she had wanted him there. She fell silent.

He ignored the implication. 'I slept better than I have in a long time, knowing that the financial future of my property is secure. Thank you.' The last words were heartfelt, and the intimacy of them shocked her.

'You're welcome.' She was in the bed of an incredibly handsome man, and he was thanking her. 'And thank you. For yesterday. For everything.'

He smiled, which was almost as blinding as the sunlight. Why must he be so beautiful, even in the morning? A night sleeping upright in a chair had not diminished the grace of his movements or dented his good humour. And his hair looked as fine tousled by sleep as it did when carefully combed.

She dreaded to think how she must appear: pale and groggy, hair every which way, and squinting at him without her glasses. She reached for them, knocking them off the night table, and he snatched them out of the air before they hit the floor and handed them to her, then offered the other hand to help her from bed.

She dodged it, and climbed unaided to the floor, pulling on her glasses.

'It will be all right, I think,' he said, ignoring her slight. 'We have survived our first day in London as man and wife. It will be easier from now on.'

Perhaps he was right. She went through the door to her own room to find it bustling with activity. Her clothing had arrived, and an overly cheerful girl named Molly was arranging a day dress for her, and had a breakfast tray warming by the fire. When she went downstairs, the first crates of books had arrived and were waiting for her in the sitting room. She had marked the ones that she expected to be the most important, opened those, and left the others lined up against a wall to obscure the decorating. The rest she could arrange on the shelves that had held the china figurines. She handed them, one piece at a time, to a horrified Jem to carry to storage, until his arms were quite full of tiny blushing courtiers, buxom maid servants and shepherds who seemed more interested in china milkmaids than in china sheep.

Jem appeared torn, unable to decide if he was more horrified by the overt femininity of the things or the possibility that he might loose his grip and smash several hundred pounds' worth of antique porcelain.

She waved him away, insisting that it mattered not, as long as they were gone from the room and she could have the shelves empty.

She gestured with the grouping in her hand, only to glance at the thing and set it down again on the table, rather than handing it to the overloaded servant. The statue was of a young couple in court clothes from the previous century. The man was leaning against a carefully wrought birdcage, and had caught his lover around the waist, drawing her near. She was leaning into him, bosom pressed to his shoulder, her hand cupping his face, clearly on the verge of planting a kiss on to his upturned lips.

And Penny's mind flashed back to the previous evening, and the feel of her husband's hands as they had touched her back. What would have happened if she had turned and pressed her body to his?

Jem shifted from foot to foot in the doorway, and she heard the gentle clink of porcelain.

'Never mind,' she said. 'You have more than enough to carry. I will keep this last one for now. Perhaps it can serve as a bookend.' She placed it back on the shelf, pushing it to the side to support a stack of books. *The Maid of Hamlet. The Orphan of the Rhine.* She'd kept the Minerva novels. Her lust-crazed Germans were supporting a shelf full of fainting virgins.

She sank back on to a chair, defeated by rampant romance.

There was a commotion in the hall, breaking through the silence of the room, and coming closer as she listened, as though a door had opened and a dinner party had overflowed its bounds. She could hear laughter, both male and female, and her husband by turns laughing and attempting to quiet the others.

At last there was a knock on the closed door of her room before Adam opened it and said with amused exasperation, 'Penelope, my friends wish to meet you.'

She did not know how she imagined the nobility might behave, but it had never been like this. The crowd pushed past the duke and into the room without waiting for permission to enter. The women giggled and pulled faces at the great piles of books, and one man leaned against a pile of open crates, nearly upending them on to the floor. Only the last to enter offered her anything in way of apology: he gave an embarrassed shrug that seemed to encompass the bad manners of his friends while saying that there was little he could do about it one way or the other.

'So this is where you've been keeping her, trapped in the sitting room with all these dusty books.' A pretty blonde woman in an ornate, flowered bonnet ran a critical finger over her library.

'Really, Barbara—' the laugh in Adam's response sounded false '—you make it sound as though I have her locked in her room. I am not *keeping* her anywhere.'

'She is keeping you, more like.' An attractive redhead made the comment, and Penny stiffened.

The woman clarified. 'I imagine the bonds of new love are too strong to break away, Adam. I wonder if you will manage to leave your house.'

Penny returned her cold smile. That had not been what she'd meant at all. It had been a slight on her wealth, followed by sarcasm. She was sure of it.

But Adam ignored it, smiling as if nothing had been said, and Penny vowed to follow his example.

Her husband gestured to his friends. 'Penelope, may I present Lord John and Lady Barbara Minton, Sir James and Lady Catherine Preston and my oldest, and dearest, friend, Lord Timothy Colton, and his wife, the Lady Clarissa.' He gestured to the cruel redhead and the man who had acknowledged Penny earlier. Adam smiled proudly at the man, and then looked to Penny. 'You will get along well with Tim, I think, for he is also a scholar. Botany. Horticulture. Plants and such. No idea what he's doing half the time. Quite beyond me. But I am sure it is very important.' Adam waved his hand dismissively, and Tim laughed.

Penny didn't understand the reason for her husband's pretended ignorance or the meaning of the joke. But clearly it was an old one, for the others found it most amusing. The room dissolved in mirth. It was like finding herself in a foreign land, where everyone spoke a language that she could not comprehend.

When their laughter had subsided, Clarissa spoke again. 'And what shall we call you?' The woman reached out to her, and took both her hands in what seemed to be a welcoming grip. Her fingers were ice cold.

'I know,' said Lady Barbara. 'We could call you Pen. For Adam says you like to write. And you were a book printer's daughter.'

Lady Catherine rolled her eyes. 'You write on paper, Bunny. Not in books.'

Clarissa looked down at Penny with a venomous smile. 'Surely not "Penny", for you are not so bright as all that.' There was a dangerous pause. 'Your hair, silly. It is I who should be called Penny.' She released Penny's hands and touched a coppery curl, smiling past her to look at Adam.

Penny watched, with a kind of distant fascination. Clarissa's gesture had been blatant flirtation, and she seemed not to care who noticed it. Yet her husband, Timothy, paid it no attention. He seemed more interested in the books on the table before him than his wife's behaviour to another man.

Adam ignored it as well, avoiding Clarissa's gaze while answering, 'But it is not your name, is it, Clare? Penny was named for the loyal wife of Odysseus. And she is worth far more than copper.'

There was an awkward pause.

Clarissa responded, 'So we assumed. We can hope that you are worth your weight in gold, Pen, for you will need to be to equal your husband's spending.'

And then they all laughed.

One, two, three… Penny felt shame colouring her skin compounded by anger at Clarissa and her own husband, and the pack of jackals that he had allowed into her study to torment her. She wanted nothing more than to run from the room, but it would only have made the situation worse. So she forced a laugh as well.

Her response would not have mattered, for now that she had wounded, Clarissa ignored her again and returned her attention to the duke. 'Darling Adam, it is so good to see you back amongst us. It is never the same when you are not here. London is frightfully boring without you, is it not, Timothy?'

Her own husband was looking at her with a sardonic twist to his smile. 'Would that you found such pleasure in my company as you do in Adam's, my darling.' He turned to Adam. 'But I missed you as well, old friend. Without you, times have been sober, as have I. We must put an end to that sorry condition as soon as possible. White's? Boodle's? Name your poison, as they say.'

'White's, I think. This evening?'

'Of course.'

Clarissa stamped her foot. 'You will do nothing of the kind. I expect you to dine in this evening. With us.' She made little effort to include her husband in her invitation. And none to include Penny, literally turning away to shut her out from the group.

Adam eluded her gaze again, speaking to the room rather than the woman before him. 'We would, but I believe my wife has other plans.' There was the subtlest emphasis on 'we', to remind Clarissa of the change in status. And then he glanced at Penny, waiting for her to confirm what he had said.

She tried to imagine herself responding as Clarissa had. She would say something clever, about how divine it would be to spend an evening at table with a woman who her husband held so dear. And there would be the same ironic tone that the others were using, to indicate an undercurrent of flirtation, and proof that she knew what was what. It would anger Adam, but he would admire her fearlessness. And it would enrage Clarissa. Which would be strangely pleasing, for Penny found herself taking an instant dislike to the woman.

Instead, she replied haltingly, 'Yes, I fear I am most busy. With my studies. And will be unable to get away.'

'You cannot leave your books.' Clarissa turned and

glanced down at her, then looked back at the others as if Penny's social ineptitude had been more than confirmed. 'But you do not mind if Adam comes without you, of course.' The woman dared her to respond in the negative.

And here was where she must admit defeat, ceding the field with the battle barely begun. Although why she would feel the need to fight for this, she had no idea.

Before she could answer, Adam spoke for her. 'My darling wife would have my best interests at heart, no matter what she might say, for she wishes to see me happy. And since I have already expressed a desire to go to White's with Tim, she would not think to drag me into mixed society, no matter how pleasant it might be for her.' He glanced back to his friend. 'Eight o'clock, then?'

If Tim was relieved, he did not show it, only smiling in acknowledgement of the plan. And then he smiled at Penny with unexpected warmth. 'Do not worry, my dear. No gels allowed at White's. I will keep your new husband on the straight and narrow. As long as you have no objection to cards and whisky.'

Penny searched again for a clever reply that would not come. 'Of course, not. Whatever Adam wishes…'

Clarissa was clearly piqued. 'It does not do, Penelope, to give a man latitude in these things. It leads them to take one too much for granted.'

Adam snapped back at her, 'On the contrary, Clarissa, a man is more likely to give his affection to one who can manage, on occasion, to put the needs of others before her own selfish desires.' Adam was looking straight into the woman's eyes for once, and

Penny realised, with sickening clarity, why he had been avoiding the contact.

They were lovers. They had been, or soon would be—it mattered not which. While Adam might smile at the wives of the other men in the room and laugh at their foolishness, he dared not acknowledge Clarissa, for when he looked at her, the guilt was plain in his eyes for all who cared to see.

After the brief lapse, he looked away from her again, and proceeded to act as though she were not in the room with them.

Penny looked to the others, watching the silent messages flash between them. Those who were positioned to see Adam's expression passed the truth to those who could not, with furtive glances and hungry smiles. Only Timothy appeared oblivious to what had happened, his attention absorbed by a volume of Aristotle.

And then the moment passed, and Adam stepped around Clarissa to stand behind his own wife. 'I am lucky to have married such a gracious woman, and hope never to take the fact for granted.'

Penny felt the mortification rising in her, forming a barrier between her and the outside. Was she expected to put her needs so far to the side that she must condone his adultery?

And then her husband put his hand upon her shoulder, as a gesture of affection and solidarity, and she jumped, as though she had been burned.

There were more sidelong glances and more wicked smiles. Suddenly Lord Timothy cut through the silence, shutting his book with a snap. 'Yes, Adam. We must offer you congratulations on your amazing luck. And it is good that you recognise it, for a man is truly blessed when he has the love and respect of such an intelligent woman.' He turned to the others in his party. 'And now, ladies and gentleman, we should be going, for we are quite destroying the peace of the household and keeping her Grace from her studies.'

'Let me show you out.' Adam took the lead, and the others fell obediently in behind him. Clarissa made as if to stay behind, but her husband held the door for her, making it impossible for her to linger.

When she was gone, Lord Timothy turned back into the room, and favoured Penny with another brief, encouraging smile. 'Good day to you, Penelope. And good fortune as well.' And then he was gone, shutting the door behind him.

She sank back on to the settee, weak with confusion. Adam had seemed so kind. He was good to her. Affectionate, in a distant sort of way. And in a short time it had become easy to imagine the affection blossoming into something warmer. Never passion. She could not hope for something so ridiculous. But love, in the classical sense. A respect for each other that might lead to a mutually satisfying relationship.

But how could she ever trust a man that would betray his best friend? And what did he mean for her, in any case? They had talked in Scotland about living as amiable strangers. And then he had paraded his lover under her nose, allowed her to be the butt of his friends' jokes, then glossed it over with fine and empty words about mutual respect.

If this was how fashionable society behaved, then she had been right in her decision to turn her back on it. But what was she to do if society hunted her out and continued to harass her?

She could hear her husband's step in the hall, and prayed that, for once, he would abide by his earlier promises, go to his study, and leave her in peace.

But instead he opened her door without preamble and shut it tightly behind him, then glared at her. He was angry. She could see it flashing in his eyes, and noted the stiffness of his back, as though his movements were containing some sudden physical outburst. His tone was curt. 'I wish to speak of what just happened here.'

'Nothing happened, as far as I noticed.'

'Exactly.' He frowned. 'And those around us took note of the nothing. It will be quite the talk of the town.'

'They took note of so many things, I am at a loss as to which one you refer to. Could it have been when you informed them of my monetary worth to you?'

'I misspoke. I had intended to praise your virtues, and the words went wrong.'

'Perhaps because I have so few virtues to extol. Since you cannot discuss my birth or my beauty, I should thank you on the compliment to my purse.'

'Believe me, Penny, I do not wish to call further attention to your wealth. It is not a point of pride that my friends suspect I married beneath me to get to your money.'

'Beneath you?' she snapped. 'When I discovered you, you were face down in a stable yard and under the horses. To marry beneath yourself, you would have to look quite a bit further than the daughter of a cit. There was not much lower you could have sunk.'

He flinched. 'I will avoid fulsome praise of you in the future, for I have no talent for flattery. In any case, it is wasted on one who makes no attempt to hide her distaste of me.'

'*I* have a distaste of you? Whatever do you mean?'

He glared at her. 'I might have been face down in the muck when you found me, but in marrying me, you got control of your inheritance and bagged a title. You understand, do you not, that many men would not be nearly so tractable as I have been towards you? We get on quite well, considering. And I did not mean to insult you in any way, nor do I plan to in the future. But I expect the same in return.

'It is one thing, madam, to refuse my affection, when we are alone. You avoided my hand this morning, but I thought, "Perhaps she is shy. I must give her time to trust me." But it is quite another thing to shrink from my merest touch when we are in public.'

'I did nothing of the kind.'

He reached to touch her hand, and she pulled away from him.

He smiled, coldly. 'Of course not, my dear. You are just as welcoming now as you were before. I touched your shoulder, and you looked to all the world as if I had struck you.'

'I thought it was agreed—'

'When I agreed to a marriage in name only, I did not realise that you found me so utterly repugnant that you would deny me all physical contact. Nor did I expect that you would make the fact known to my friends.'

'You do not repel me.' No matter how much she might wish he did.

'Oh, really? Then you had best prove it to me. Take my hand and assure me.'

She stared at the hand he held out to her, the long fingers curled to beckon, but she made no move to take it.

He nodded. 'I see. Most comforting.'

'I do not see why it is so important to you.' *You have her attention. Why must you have mine as well?*

He stared back at her until she met his eyes. 'I am a proud man. I do not deny it. It does not reflect well on either of us to have the full details of our relationship as public gossip. We are married, and I hope to remain so. The time will pass more easily for both of us if you can bring yourself to be at ease in my company, at least when we are in public. I will not bother you at home any more than is necessary.'

There was frustration and anger in his eyes, but they were still the same compelling blue, and just as hard to resist as they had been when she had trusted his motives. 'How can I do this?' she asked herself, as much as she did him.

His shoulders relaxed a little. 'You could, on occasion, smile while in public. I would not expect unceasing mirth. Merely as pleasant a face as you wear when we are alone. And if my hand should happen to brush yours, you need not flinch from it.' He raised his hand in oath. 'I promise to treat you with the care and respect due my wife and my duchess.' And then he offered it to her again.

She closed her eyes, knowing in her heart what his respect for his wife was worth, if he could not respect the marriage of another. Then she reached tentatively out to put her hand in his.

She heard him sigh, and his fingers closed over hers, stroking briefly before pushing her hand back until they were palm to palm and he could link fingers with her. He squeezed. 'There. Feel? There is nothing to be afraid of. I mean you no harm.' His other hand came to her face, and the fingertips brushed lightly against her cheek. 'I only wish for you to leave others with the impression that there is some warm feeling between us. Nothing more. That perhaps we might share something other than an interest in your money. Help me undo my foolish words.' His hand touched her hair and stroked to the back of her neck, and he moved close enough so she could feel his breath on her skin, and the change in the air against her lips as he spoke.

'This is much better, is it not?' His voice was low and husky, as she had never heard it before, barely more than a whisper.

She opened her eyes. He was right. When he was this close and looking at her, it ceased to matter how he looked at other women. She could feel the magnetic pull to be even closer. She had but to lean in a few inches, and his lips would be upon hers.

Which was madness. She had to resist yet another urge to jump away from him in alarm, and watched as his pupils shrank, and the soft smile on his face returned to its normal, more businesslike form. He withdrew slowly, with easy, unruffled grace. 'Very good. That is much more what I had hoped for. I do not expect you to fall passionately into my arms as a false display for visitors. But if we could at least give the appearance that we are on friendly terms, I would be most grateful.' His fingers untwined and his hand slipped away from hers.

'Most certainly. For I do wish to be on friendly terms with you in more than appearance.' She sighed, and hoped it sounded like a longing for her books, and not for renewed contact. 'And now, if you will excuse me? I must return to work.'

'Of course.'

Adam left the room, closing the door behind him, and moved quickly down the hall. Hell and damnation, it had been an unbearable morning. First, the invasion of his friends, before he'd had a chance to explain to Penny how things were likely to be. Although she probably suspected, what with the way Clarissa had been making a fool of herself, with no care for the fact that Tim was in the room with them.

Penny must think him a complete fraud. She had looked around the room, at his friends and at Clarissa, and had seen it all. She'd read his character in a glance and must regret her decision.

And he, who had always been so sure of his words, even when nothing else would go right for him, had stumbled so egregiously as to let it appear that he had married her for money. If possible, it was even worse than the truth to say such a thing. He had allowed her no dignity at all. And he had seen the mocking light in the eyes of his friends when she had flinched from his touch.

He had been foolishly angry, at himself and at Clarissa, and had taken it out on Penny for not offering affection that he had not earned. But what had he been about, just now? Had he been trying to teach her some kind of lesson? Hopefully, it had been lost on her, if he had. He should have come back to her and taken her hand in a most friendly fashion, and tried to mend the breach he had caused. He should have assured her that although he had been guilty of grave transgressions, it was all in the past, and that he meant to be a better man.

Instead, he had touched her hair and forgotten all. What sense was it to talk when there were soft lips so close, waiting to be kissed? And she had closed her eyes so sweetly, allowing him to observe the fine lashes and the smooth cheek and the sweetness of her breath as it mingled with his. It was a matter of inches, a bare nod of the head to bring them into contact with his own, and to slip his tongue into her mouth and kiss her until she reacted to his touch with the eagerness he expected in a wife.

He shook his head again. Had he forgotten whom he was speaking of? If he needed to persuade his own wife to let him hold her hand, then passion-drugged nights were not likely to be in the offing.

Not while he remained at home, at any rate. Perhaps it had been too long since last he visited his mistress. A man had urges, after all. And he was neglecting his if his own wife began to tempt him more than someone else's. An afternoon relaxing in the arms of his paramour would clear his mind, which was clouded with misdirected lust, and make it easier to decide what to do about the impossible relationship with Clarissa and the unwelcome attraction to Penelope.

He called for a carriage and set out to regain control of his emotions.

As he passed out the door, he saw Penny's manservant, who stood at the entrance to the house, wearing the Bellston livery as though it were as great an honour as a night in the stocks. He looked at Adam and bowed with as much respect as the other servants, while conveying the impression that the lady of the house was worth two dukes.

Adam glared back at him. 'Jem, isn't it?'

'Yes, your Grace.' And another bow.

Damn the man. Adam fished in his pocket and came up with a handful of banknotes and forced them into the servant's hand. 'I have an errand for you. Go to the bookseller's. And buy my wife that damned copy of Homer.'

Chapter Nine

In the two years they had been together, Adam's mistress, Felicity, had been a most accommodating and entertaining companion. But now, as he looked at her, he could not seem to remember why. She was beautiful, of course. There was little reason to have her otherwise. While she might not be the most enchanting conversationalist, he employed her to listen, not to talk. And so it mattered little.

She greeted him as she always had, with a passionate kiss. Her perfect hands reached out to stroke him and to smooth his brow.

And to search his pockets, as well. 'What did you being me, Adam?' Her smile was as satisfied as a cat's.

He smiled back. 'And why must I have brought you anything?' Although, of course, he had.

'Because you always do, my darling. I have come to expect it. And there is the little matter of your recent marriage.' She experimented with a pout, but her heart was not in it. 'You could at least have told me your plans. Even though it does not change what we share, it is not pleasant to be surprised when reading *The Times*.'

He nodded. 'I am sorry. I never intended for my situation to change so suddenly, or I would have fore-warned you.'

She nodded. 'It was love at first sight, then.' Clearly, she did not believe it any more than he did, but it was sweet of her to give him the benefit of the doubt.

'Rather. Yes.'

'Then, let us celebrate.' She kissed him again with an ardour guaranteed to arouse.

But the irony of the situation washed over him, and it was as though he were watching the kiss from a distance, rather than being an active participant in it. To be celebrating one's wedding in the arms of a Cyprian was probably sin enough for God to strike him dead on the spot. When their lips parted, he laid his against her ear and murmured, 'Then you no longer wish to see your gift?'

'I wish to see it, if you wish to show it to me,' she said, the most co-operative woman in his life.

He guided her fingers to the breast pocket of his jacket, to the package he had purchased on the way to her flat.

She was immediately distracted and withdrew the bracelet from the jewel box in his pocket. 'Adam, it is magnificent. The size of the diamonds. And the clarity.' She examined it with the eye of a professional. 'Th-thank you. It is quite the nicest thing you have ever brought me.'

He must have chosen well, if he had made a whore stammer. 'I am glad you appreciate it.'

For it cost me more than all your other gifts put together. Now that I can borrow from my wife's purse, money does not matter. And she will not care that I am here, for I have bought her a book. The truth sickened him, even as he thought it. And again, it was as though he was viewing the scene from a distance.

His mind might be shamed by what he had done, but his body cared not, and awaited the reward forthcoming after a gift.

And his mouth agreed with neither of them. As though he had no control over it, it announced, 'Yes. Of course. I thought, under the circumstances, an extra expenditure was called for. For you see…'

And his mouth proceeded, unbidden, to explain that now that he was married, their relationship had indeed changed. Since it was unlikely that he would be able to spend much time in her presence, it was hardly fair to keep her. The lavish gift was meant as a parting token. The apartment would be available for her use until such time…

His body howled in disappointment, and called him all kinds of fool, but still the words would not stop. And with each one, his conscience felt lighter.

His mistress was taking the whole thing annoyingly well.

She shrugged. 'I suspected as much. When a man gets it into his head to marry, his priorities change. And we have been together for quite some time, have we not?'

He started. She sounded bored with his attentions. The fact that she bored him as well was small consolation.

'And you have always been most considerate of me, and very generous of spirit. Should you need similar companionship in the future, I would not hesitate to recommend you as a protector.'

It sounded almost as if she was giving him references. 'And I, you.' He stuttered. 'Recommend, I mean. Should you need…'

He returned to his townhouse, numb with shock. The day was not turning out as planned. His old friends annoyed him. He'd just denied himself an afternoon of pleasure for no logical reason. And he still had no idea how to deal with his new wife. He returned home, because he could think of nowhere else to go. There was no joy in lunching alone, but his clubs would be too full of people, asking questions he did not desire to answer. At least in his own house he could have the consolation of solitude.

He was over the threshold before he remembered that he no longer lived alone. He had handed his hat and stick to the servant, and was halfway down the hall when he heard the rattle of tea things from the sitting room. Her door was open.

Too late, then, to take back his hat and back out of the door. Perhaps she would not notice if he quietly went to his rooms.

And then his wife peered into the hall. 'I was just sitting down to tea. Would you care to join me?'

'Thank you.' Once again, his mouth had said something that came as a surprise to him.

'I will have the butler bring another cup. You look in

need of refreshment. Come. Sit down.' And she graciously welcomed him to sit in his own home.

Her home as well, he reminded himself. She had every right to be taking tea in the room he had promised was solely for her use. And she was performing her duty as wife to see that he was provided with his. What right did he have to complain?

He sat down on the sofa next to her and waited in silence, while she pulled a tiny table closer to him and prepared his cup as she'd seen him take it. 'Biscuit?'

He stared at the unfamiliar thing in front of him.

She responded without his asking, 'I am accustomed to take sweets in the afternoon. These are a favourite of mine. I find the lemon zest in them most refreshing, so I have given the recipe to Cook. But if you would prefer something more substantial…'

'No. This is fine. Thank you.'

She was staring at him now. And he raised his eyes from his cup, to stare back at her.

'I am sorry for suggesting it,' she remarked, 'but is something the matter? You seem rather out of sorts.'

'What business is it of yours?' he snapped. And immediately regretted his outburst.

She was unfazed. 'Only that, earlier in the day, you said you wished to be friends.'

'I said I wished to appear to be friends. That is an entirely different matter.'

Again, she was unfazed, but answered thoughtfully, 'As you wish. Although it is sometimes easier to keep up the appearance, if an actual friendship exists.' There was no tartness in her voice. Merely a statement of fact.

He rubbed his brow with his hand. 'I apologise. Of course, you are right. I had no call to snap at you.'

'As you wish. I was not offended by it. It is I who should apologise to you for intruding on your peace. I merely wished to thank you for sending Jem to get my book. It was nice that you remembered.' She fell silent and allowed him to enjoy his tea.

But the silence was almost more discomforting than the noise, for it allowed him to feel the guilt again, although he could not imagine what it was that pained him.

'You are not disturbing my peace, Penny. But I fear I disturbed yours. I think—it may be possible that I am not comfortable when at peace. I must always be doing something to keep back the quiet. Thus, I released my ill-behaved friends on you this morning.'

She chuckled. 'We are an unsuitable pair, are we not?'

'Opposites attract.' But he could not manage to sound as sure as he wished.

'But at least our political views agree. It would be most difficult to respect you if—'

'Our politics?' It was his turn to laugh. 'To what purpose does a woman have political views?'

'To no purpose, other than that I live in this country, and am concerned with how it progresses. While I am not allowed to vote, there is nothing to prevent me from reading the speeches and governmental proceedings in *The Times*. That I cannot do anything to forward my views is no fault of mine.' She cast her eyes downwards, and then favoured him with a sidelong glance through her lashes. 'As a weak woman, I must pray that the country is in good hands.'

He felt the small thrill along his spine that he always got when a woman was trying to capture his attention. Could it be? He looked at her again. There was a faint smile on her face, and an even fainter flush on her pale skin.

His wife was flirting with him. Over the proceedings of the House of Lords.

It was an unusual approach, and unlikely to be successful. It would be easy enough to prove that she knew nothing of the subject with a few simple questions. And then, if she truly wished to flatter him, she could return to safer subjects favoured by other women of his female acquaintance: the colour of his eyes, or the cut of his coat and how well it favoured his shoulders. 'So you agree with my politics, do you?'

'Most definitely. Your grasp of economy is most erudite.'

'And you feel that the country is competently governed? For having seen the political process up close, I sometimes have my doubts.'

'Well, as far as I can tell, Lord Beaverton is a fool,' she said. 'He has little understanding of domestic trade, and even less of international issues. And he seems to disagree most vehemently with you on the subject of cotton imports.'

'Because he has interests in India,' Adam supplied. 'He is feathering his own nest.'

'Well, your interchange with him sounded most spirited. Although, if you could clarify a certain point...'

He had wondered when she would allow him to

speak, for she seemed to have no understanding of the conversational gambit that encouraged a woman to listen more than she spoke. Her first question was followed by another, and then another. And some were of a level of complexity that he was required to refer to a gazetteer in his study, and other references as well.

And soon it seemed easier just to move the tea things and conversation to his desk. He ceded her the chair, for he sometimes found it easier to think while on his feet, and she peppered him with questions while he paced the room.

There was a discreet knock at the door, and the butler entered. 'Your Grace? You have guests.'

A head appeared around the back of the servant. Tim was there, and he could see other friends crowding behind him in the hall. 'Have you forgotten, Adam? Dinner at the club?'

He glanced at the clock on the mantel. How had it got to be so late? 'It will be the work of a moment, and I will be ready to go.' He glanced down at Penny. 'Of course, if you wish, I will cancel.'

She shook her head. 'That is all right. I prefer to remain at home.' He thought he detected a trace of wistfulness in her answer.

'If you are sure?'

She nodded again, gathering her tea things from his desk. 'I should be going back to my room, after all. I meant to accomplish more today.'

'I am sorry if I distracted you. Until tomorrow, then.' And before he knew what he was doing, he'd bent and kissed her on the cheek.

She turned as pink as the walls of her sitting room, but she did not flinch from him. In fact, the smile he received in reward was quite charming, before she remembered that there were others present, and hurried across the hall and into her study, closing the door.

In retrospect, he'd have been better to have remained at home, for that seemed to be where his mind resided. The strange day only served to accent the commonness of the evening. The boring conversation and stale jokes of his friends were punctuated with exclamations of 'Adam, why must you be so glum?'

The constant reminder that he was not himself only served to make his mood darker.

When they were at cards, and Minton had presented some outlandish political position, Adam had snapped, 'Really, John, if I wished to talk politics, I'd have stayed home with my wife. She, at least, has some idea of what she is talking about.'

There was an amused murmur in the crowd around him, as though he had confirmed to the men around him that his sudden marriage had addled his mind. Only Tim looked at him and nodded with approval.

Soon after, a servant arrived, bearing a note on a salver for Tim. His friend unfolded the paper, grew pale, and asked a servant for his hat and gloves. 'I must make my apologies. I am called home. There is an emergency.'

'Nothing serious, I hope,' Adam said.

'I suspect it is little Sophie. She has been sick again. And I am a little worried.' Judging by Tim's agitation, minor worry did not describe his true state of mind.

Adam stood up. 'I will go with you. We will take my carriage to save time, and I will return home once your mind is at rest.'

But on arrival at the Colton home, they discovered the true nature of the emergency. All the lights were blazing, and from the salon came the sound of voices, laughter, and a soprano warbling along with the pianoforte.

Tim swore softly and with vehemence threw his hat into a corner and stalked into the room with Adam following in his wake.

His wife seized him by the arm, forcing a drink into his hand and announced to the gathering, 'Here they are! As I told you, they were detained.'

Adam was close enough to hear Tim murmur to his wife, 'You knew my intentions, and yet you brought me home to play host to a gathering that is none of my making.'

She responded through clenched teeth. 'And you knew my intentions. I wished for you and your friend to dine at home this evening. Do not cross me again, or you shall live to regret it.'

'More so than I do our marriage?' Tim laughed loud enough for the guests to hear, although they could not make out his words. 'That would be an impressive feat, madam.'

'You know how creative I can be.' She turned away from Tim, and reached for Adam, linking her arm in his and pulling him forwards. 'Come along, Adam. Do not think you can escape so easily. Have a drink with us before you go.' She was pressing against him in a way that must be obvious to her husband, and smiling up at him too brightly.

He eased free of her grasp, stomach churning, unable to look his friend in the eye. 'A glass of wine, then. Only one. And then I must be going home.'

Clarissa said, loud enough for all to hear, 'Ah yes. Hurrying home to your bride, Adam. Just when will she be making an appearance in society? People are beginning to think that the woman is a product of your over-heated imagination.'

'You know full well, Clare, that she wished to remain at home, for you spoke to her this morning.'

'But, Adam, everyone is dying to meet her. I have told them so much about her. They are aflame with curiosity. Penelope is the daughter of a cit,' she informed the group gathered around them. 'And from what I've been told, she is very rich. But she will not mix with us, I'm afraid. She is far too busy to be bothered. Adam's wife is a bluestocking.' The last was said with enough pity to make the other revelations pale in comparison.

He was expected to say something at this point, but was at a loss as to what. Most of what Clarissa had said was perfectly true, although it sounded far worse coming from her mouth. And she had probably used his absence to embroider what facts she had with as many scurrilous fictions as she could invent. So he seized upon the one thing he could safely refute. 'Really, Clarissa. You make her sound so exclusionist that she should be a patroness at Almack's. She is at home tonight, reading *The Odyssey* in the original Greek. I bought her the book this afternoon as a wedding gift. But she'll mix with society soon enough.'

And then, he could not help himself—he added a fabrication of his own. 'We are planning a ball, and I suspect most of you will be invited to it. Then you can meet her and see for yourself.'

The crowd nodded, mollified, and there was an undercurrent of curiosity in the gossip that stole the thunder from Clarissa's tales. Bellston rarely entertained. The new duchess might be an eccentric, but no one would dare comment on the fact if it meant losing the duke's favour and missing a chance to attend an event that would be eagerly anticipated by everyone of importance in London.

Everyone except the Duchess of Bellston.

Penny sat at the vanity in her bedroom, which she had transformed, with the help of a strong lamp, into a makeshift writing desk. The work had seemed to fly this evening, with words flowing out of her mind and on to paper as easily as if the text were already in English and she was only copying down what she saw. Perhaps it had been the gift of the book that had inspired her. Adam could be so effortlessly kind that she scolded herself for thinking ill of him earlier in the day.

Or perhaps the intellectual stimulation of strong tea and good conversation had freed her thoughts.

That was all it had been, of course. Any stimulation she might have felt, beyond her intellect, was girlish fancy. She had always admired the Duke of Bellston. To see the actual man in front of her, moved by his subject matter until he'd all but forgotten her existence, was more invigorating than she'd imagined. He'd invited her into his study, allowing her past a barrier of intimacy that she had not expected to cross, and for a time she'd felt she was very much in his confidence.

And then he had kissed her. Thank the Lord that their conversation had been at an end, for she doubted that she would have been able to string two thoughts together after that buss on the cheek.

She had gone back to her sitting room and curled up on the sofa and opened the book, ready to enjoy his gift, only to have her eyes drawn, again and again, to the kissing couple on the bookshelf. She must have looked as dazed and eager as that when he'd left her.

And it had not stopped him from going out, she reminded herself, returning to cool logic. Not that there was anything wrong with being apart in the evenings. How would she get any work done if he forced her to accompany him everywhere, like a dog on a leash? She enjoyed her work.

And she had been quite satisfied with her progress once she left the sitting room, which seemed to attract foolish fantasy like a normal library attracted cobwebs. She could work without fear of interruption in her bedroom.

Certainly without fear of interruption by her husband. If he preferred to be elsewhere, in the company of others than herself? That had been their plan, had it not? She could hardly blame him for it. An evening of cards at an all-male club was hardly cause for jealousy on her part.

And if she was not mistaken, he was arriving home; through the open window she heard the sound of a carriage stopping in front of the house, and the faint sound of her husband's voice as the footman greeted him at the front door. She glanced at the clock. Barely eleven.

She had not expected him so soon. It had been later than this when they'd returned to the house on the previous evening, and he'd proclaimed it early. Was tonight's behaviour unusual?

Not that she should care. She hardly knew the man, and his schedule was his own affair.

But he had come home. Not to her, precisely. But he was home, all the same. Perhaps it would not be too forward to go downstairs in search of a cup of tea, and pass by the door to his study to see if he remained up. She got out of her chair, reached to tighten the belt of her dressing gown, and, without thinking, straightened her hair. Then she laughed at herself for the vanity of it.

With her hand on the doorknob, she stopped and listened. But, no. There was no need to seek him. He was climbing the stairs, for she could hear him on the landing, and then he was coming down the hall carpet toward his room. She waited for the sound of his bedroom door, opening and closing.

It did not come. He had walked past his room, for she had been unconsciously counting the steps and imagining him as he walked.

And then he stopped, just on the other side of her door. She waited for the knock, but none came. Perhaps he would call out to her, to see if she was asleep, though he must know she was not, for the light of her lamp would be visible under the door.

If she were a brave woman, she would simply open the door and go after the cup of tea she had been imagining. Then she could pretend to be surprised to see him, and inquire what it was that he wanted. She might even step into the hall, and collide with his body, allowing him to reach out a hand to steady her. Perhaps he would laugh, and she would neglect to step away, and she would know if he merely wished to continue their discussion, or if there was some other purpose for his visit.

But she was not a brave woman, and she was foolish to think such things, since they made no sense at all. There was a perfectly logical explanation for his being there, which he would no doubt tell her in the morning at breakfast. If she waited, she could save herself the embarrassment of making too big a thing out of something so small.

But all the same, she kissed the palm of her hand, and then silently pressed it to the panel of the door, holding it very near where the cheek of a tall man might be.

Then she heard his body shift, and his steps retreating down the hall, and the opening and closing of the bedroom door beside her own.

Chapter Ten

When she woke the next morning, she found herself listening for sounds from the next room and hoping for a knock on the connecting door. Surely Adam would come to her as soon as he was awake, and explain his behaviour the previous evening?

But she heard only silence. Perhaps he was a late sleeper, or simply did not wish to be disturbed.

When she could stand to wait no longer, she called for her maid. She would go downstairs and wait for him at breakfast. But when she arrived in the breakfast room, she was told that his Grace had been up for hours, had had a light meal and gone riding in the park.

Very well, then. If he had wished to speak to her, it had been nothing of importance. Or perhaps she had only imagined it, for things often sounded different through a closed door. Whatever the case, she would go on with her day as if nothing had happened.

She gathered her papers from her bedroom and

returned them to the sitting room, where the morning light made working easier. And in daylight, with her husband nowhere about, there seemed to be fewer romantic fantasies clouding her mind. But to avoid temptation, she turned the figurine of the lovers to face the wall.

She had barely opened her books before there was a quiet knock on the door, and a servant announced a visitor, offering a card on a tray.

Lady Clarissa Colton.

The card lay there on the tray before her, like a dead snake. What was she to do about it? 'Tell the lady that Adam is not at home.'

The servant looked pained. 'She wished specifically for you, your Grace.'

'Then tell her I am not—'

'Hello.' Clarissa was calling to her from the hall. She laughed. 'You must forgive me, darling. I have viewed this as a second home for so long that I quite forget my manners.'

'I see.' Penny had hoped to load those words with censure. But instead they sounded like understanding and permission to enter, for Clarissa pushed past the servant and came into the sitting room.

She sat down next to Penny, as though they were confidants. 'Adam and I are old friends. Particularly close. But I'm sure he must have told you.' Clarissa was smiling sweetly again, but her eyes were hard and cold. She reached out to take Penny's hands, giving them a painful squeeze. 'And when I heard the good news, I simply could not stay away.'

'News?'

'Yes. He told us last night, at the party. Everyone was most excited.'

'Party?' Obviously, there was much Adam had not told her. And now, she was left to parrot monosyllables back to Clarissa, until the horrible woman made the truth clear.

'Ooo, that is right. You did not know of it.' Clarissa made a face that was supposed to represent sympathy, but looked more like concealed glee. 'Adam came to our house last night after dinner. Not for the whole evening, as I had hoped. But he could not bear to disappoint me. The man is beyond kind.'

Far beyond it, as far as Penny was concerned.

'We knew you would not mind, of course, for you did not wish to come. In any case, he told us about the ball.'

'Ball?' She had done it again. Why in heaven could she not find her tongue?

'That you will be hosting, to celebrate your marriage. I am sure it will be the most divine affair. Your ballroom is magnificent, is it not? And Adam uses it far too seldom…'

Obviously, for she was not even sure of its location since her husband had neglected to show it to her. She nodded mutely, along with the flow of Clarissa's words.

'It is more than large enough to hold the cream of London society. We will begin the guest list this morning, and the menu, of course. And in the afternoon, we can see about your gown.' She glanced down at Penny's sombre grey day dress. 'I do not know what fashion was like where you came from—'

'I came from London,' Penny interjected.

'But these clothes will hardly do. We must fit you with a new wardrobe, gloves, perhaps a turban for evening. With an ostrich feather. You will adore it, I am sure.'

Penny was quite sure that she would look ridiculous with her hair dressed in plumes. And that was probably the point of the suggestion.

'We will go to my modiste, together. And I will instruct her on just how you must look, to display your true self to the world.'

There could not be a more horrifying prospect than that. Must she be polite to this woman, for the sake of her husband? Or could she say what she thought, and risk making a powerful enemy?

'Penelope. So sorry to intrude, I had no idea you were entertaining.' Adam stood in the doorway, still in his riding clothes, expression unreadable.

'That is all right, dear. You are not interrupting anything of importance. Only discussion of our ball.'

Discussion had been a charitable way to describe it. 'Clarissa says that you announced it at her home last evening. It was most unwise of you to give the secret away before we set a date.' *Or before telling your wife.*

He seemed to pale ever so slightly at being caught out. Then he regained his smile and said, 'So sorry, darling. I could not help myself.'

'Really?' They would see about that. 'No matter. Clarissa has come to offer her help in the matter, if I need it.'

Adam smiled again. 'How kind of her. But I am sure you have the matter well in hand, so she needn't have bothered.'

Clarissa laughed. 'Don't be ridiculous, Adam. She will have no experience in handling a gathering of this sort. She knows nothing of our set, or what will be expected of her. And you have thrown her into it, assuming that she will not embarrass herself. It will be a disaster.'

Penny hardly dared breathe, for fear that Clarissa would notice how close to the truth she had come.

But Adam waved his hand and shrugged. 'I doubt it is so hard as all of that, and Penny is a most enterprising and intelligent woman. No need for you to bother about it. But thank you for your concern. Let me show you out, and we will leave my wife to her work.'

'I could not think to leave the poor creature in the state she's in.' Clarissa spoke as if Penny was not in the room. 'At least convince her to leave her books long enough to go shopping, like a normal female.'

'You were going shopping, eh? Well, I know how much you enjoy that, and we mustn't keep you from it. Perhaps, some day, when Penny is finished with her book, you may come back for her. But for now…' Adam reached out a hand to her.

Clarissa weighed, just for a moment, continuing the argument against the chance to be nearer to Adam, if only for the short walk to the door. Then she smiled up at him and said, 'Very well, then. There is nothing for it—if you wish me to go, I must go.' She rose, and linked her arm with his. 'And perhaps you can be persuaded to tell me what I must purchase, so that I look my finest when I return for the ball. I do wish to look my best when in your presence.'

She watched them leave the room, Clarissa smiling brightly and leaning on Adam as if she could not manage to walk the few steps to the door without his support.

Penny did not realise that she was still clutching a pencil in her hand until the thing snapped under the pressure of her fingers. The gall of the woman. The infernal nerve. To come into her house, to point out her flaws and to rub her face in her husband's perfidy. The rage simmered in her, as she waited for Adam to return.

Before he was near enough to speak, she met him in the hall, and demanded, 'What is going on?'

'Penny. The servants.' He said it as though the lack of privacy should be sufficient to contain her temper.

But she was having none of it. 'The servants might also want to know the amount of extra work you have brought to this house, for you have certainly set us all a task. We are to have a ball, are we? Do we even have a ballroom? Clarissa seems to think so, but I do not know, myself.'

His ears turned slightly red, which might indicate embarrassment, but nothing showed in his voice. 'It is on the third floor. We have not had time for a whole tour—'

'Because we have been married less than a week. I have lived in this house for only two days, and at no time do I remember any discussion of our hosting an entertainment.'

He backed her into the sitting room, and shut the door behind them. 'The subject came up yesterday evening.'

'When you were at Clarissa's party. Another thing you made no mention of.'

'And *I* do not remember, in any of our discussions, the need to inform you of my whereabouts at all times. In fact, I specifically remember our agreeing that our social lives would remain separate.'

'An agreement which you chose to violate when you invited all of London to our house and neglected to inform me. While I can hardly complain over your choice of *entertainments* last evening, it embarrasses me when your *hostess* chooses to come to my house and make me aware of them.'

She glared at him, and watched the guilty anger rise in his face. 'I do not like what you are implying.'

'I did not think you would. But that is hardly a denial, is it?' She waited, praying that he would tell her she was wrong, and dishonoured them both by thinking such horrible things.

Instead he said coldly, 'It does not suit you to be jealous over something that was over before we even met.'

The admission, and the easy dismissal of her feelings, made her almost too sick to speak. 'I am not jealous, Adam. What cause would I have? You know that our relationship is not likely to be close enough to merit jealousy. But I am disappointed, and more than a little disgusted. I had thought you a better person than that. And to carry on in such an obvious fashion, under the very nose of a man you claim as friend...'

'Perhaps, if I had married a woman who wished to be at my side, then there would be no cause to wonder at my relationship with another man's wife.'

She laughed in amazement. 'It is all my fault, then?

That you choose to make a fool of yourself over a married woman?'

'I am not attempting to make a fool of myself. I am endeavouring, as best I can, to make our marriage seem as normal as possible to the rest of the world. But apparently I am failing—already there has been talk about you.'

'Only because Clarissa spreads it, I am sure. Better that they should talk about me than the two of you.'

He made no effort to correct her. 'If we do not appear together in public, and supremely happy, everyone will say that I am keeping you out of sight because you are an embarrassment to me.'

'What do I care what people think of me?'

'Apparently nothing, or you would not look as you do.'

One, two, three… She closed her eyes, to stop any chance of tears, and continued her counting. She had known he would say something about her looks eventually. How could he not? But she had hoped, when the time came, it would be as a casual statement of the obvious. Then she would be better prepared, and could agree and laugh the pain away. But he had been so good about not commenting. To have it thrown back in the heat of anger had taken the breath from her and her argument with it.

She made it all the way to nine and then blurted, 'If you had a problem with my looks, then you should have thrown the licence on to the fire when we were in Scotland. There is nothing I can do to my appearance to make it a match for yours. No amount of money will turn a sow's ear into a silk purse.'

He waited until she was through with her outburst, and then said, 'Do not turn soft on me, now that I need you to be strong.' There was no kindness in his voice, but neither did he seem angry. 'Our initial plan will not work. At least, not while we are in London. And so I am making another, and I expect you to obey me in it. If you do not wish to follow my advice, I will allow Clarissa to return and badger you into your new role as duchess. She is better qualified to teach you how to navigate in society than any other woman I know. But she can be amazingly stubborn and surpassingly cruel. Do you understand?'

She bit her lip and nodded.

'First, you will not, nor will I allow you in future to, refer to yourself as a sow's ear, a lost cause, wasted effort, nothing, nobody, or any of the other terms of scorn. Self-pity is your least attractive feature, and not one I wish to see displayed in my home for the duration of our marriage.'

When she was sure her eyes were dry, she opened them and glared at him.

'Very good. You look quite like a duchess when you are angry with me.'

She could not tell if he meant to be amusing, but she had no desire to laugh.

He stared down her body. 'Is all your clothing like this?'

She nodded. 'Practical. Easy to care for.'

'Dull. Ugly. Drab.'

'I put foolish things aside when my father died.'

'And how long ago was that?'

'Two years.'

'Two years,' he repeated. 'And you are still dressed in mourning. You are a bride, Penny. And to see you dressed so is an insult to me. It is as though I pulled you from weeping on a grave, and forced you to marry.'

'Very well,' she said. 'I will wear my old things. I have more than enough gowns in storage, hardly used since my come-out.'

'But they must be…' he added quickly on his fingers '…at least five years old.'

'They are not worn, so I have not needed to replace them.'

'But hardly the first stare of fashion.'

She laughed bitterly. 'As if that would matter.'

He let out a growl of exasperation. 'You listened to nothing of what I just said. Very well, then. My patience is at an end.' He seized her by the wrist and threw open the door.

She pulled her hand away. 'What do you think you are doing?'

'What someone should have done a long time ago. You are coming with me this instant, Penelope, and you will remedy the sad state of your wardrobe.'

'There is nothing wrong with the clothing I have. It is clean and serviceable.'

'And totally unfitting for the Duchess of Bellston.'

'I never asked to be the Duchess of Bellston, and I fail to see why I should be forced to conform to her needs.'

It was Adam's turn to laugh. 'You are the duchess, whether you planned it or no. When you decided to pull a stranger from the street and marry him, it never occurred to you that there might be complications?'

She sneered. 'Of course. I suspected if I was not careful that I would have a husband eager to waste my money on foolishness. I was willing to allow it to such a degree as it did not interfere with my comfort or my studies. And I was right to be concerned, for you have breached both boundaries with this request.'

As she watched, her husband became the duke to her again, drawing in his power in a way that was both intriguing and intimidating. His voice dropped to a barely audible murmur. 'Well, then. I am glad I have fulfilled your worst fears. We must set something straight, if we are to live in harmony.'

He meant to dictate to her? Reason fled her mind, and was replaced with white-hot rage. He had no right to do this, no right to tell her who she must be, if she was to be his wife at all. *One, two, three…*

'The wardrobe I am suggesting is in no way wasteful. Think of it as a uniform, nothing more. You wish to be left in peace? Then you will find it easier to deflect notice if you can play the part of a duchess with reasonable facility. The clothing I am suggesting will make this easier and not more difficult.'

Four, five, six…

'It will be expensive, but I have seen the statements from your bank, and you can most certainly afford it. If it helps, think of it as no different than you would allow me to purchase for my mistress. You had allotted an expense of this amount, hoping to keep me occupied so that you could work. Think for a moment the level of stubbornness and bullheadedness that you must project if you allow me to spend the money, but will only berate me for it if I wish to spend it on you.'

Seven, eight, nine…

'I take your silence for assent.' He rang for a servant and ordered the carriage brought round. 'I will deposit you at a modiste, and you can work out, between you, what is best done. I care not for the details, as long as the project is completed.'

Ten. And still she could not find a hole in his argument.

'And if you balk or resort to tantrums, I will throw you over my shoulder and carry you there, for you are behaving as a spoiled child over something that any other woman in the world would enjoy.'

The nerve of the man. Very well, then. She would go to the dressmaker, get a few simple gowns in the same vein as those she owned, and escape the ridiculous display that he intended for her.

She rode in silence with him, still irritated by his insistence on controlling a thing that he could know nothing about. Before her come-out, she had had more than her share of pushy dressmakers, shoe sellers and haberdashers, all eager to force her to look a way that did not make her the least bit comfortable. She had lacked the nerve to stand up to them, and had felt no different than a trained pony at the end of it, paraded about to attract a buyer.

And it had all come to naught.

The carriage pulled to a stop in front of an unassuming shop in a side street, far away from the hustle of Bond Street. Adam stepped down and held out his hand for her, but she would not take it. Unlike some women she could name, she could manage to walk without the assistance of Adam Felkirk.

The horses chose that moment to shy, and she almost fell into the street.

But her husband caught her easily, and pulled her into his arms, and safely to the ground. Then he had the gall to smile at her. 'This is what happens when you try to resist me. There is no point in it. I suggest you surrender, now.'

She glared at the shop in front of her. 'And do you come here often to purchase clothes for women? Or is this the store that Clarissa was threatening me with?'

'I have never been here before, and I have no idea where Clarissa would have had you go. This shop was frequented by my mother.' His smile turned to an evil grin. 'She decorated the sitting room that you enjoy so well. Since it does not matter to you what you wear, the fact should not bother you at all.'

She had a momentary vision of herself, clothed in bright pink organza, and could not control her grimace.

Adam nodded. 'I will leave you to it, madam, for you know best what to do. But do not think you can return home without purchases, for I am taking the carriage and the driver will not return for you for several hours.' He looked at her servant, hanging on the back of the carriage. 'I will leave Jem with you.' He tossed the man a sovereign. 'When the carriage comes back, if you can carry the purchases in one trip, she has not bought enough. Tell the driver to leave and return in another hour.'

And her own servant, who she should have been able to trust, pocketed the coin and bowed to his new master.

Adam looked to her again. 'When you are home, we will discuss the ball. Do not worry yourself about it. My mother had menus and guest lists as well. I am sure they will serve, and we can pull the whole thing together with a minimum of bother.'

Chapter Eleven

Penny watched the carriage roll away from her. Damn the man. He knew nothing about anything if he meant to pull a ball together with the help of a woman who, she suspected, had been dead far longer than her own father. Clarissa was right: it was a disaster in the making.

And what was she to do for the rest of the afternoon, trapped here? If she had known his intent was to abandon her, she'd have brought something to read. She stepped off the street and into the shop.

A girl dropped the copy of *Le Beau Monde* that she had been paging through and sprang to her feet behind a small gold desk. She said, with a thick French accent, 'May I be of assistance, your ladyship?'

The girl sounded so hopeful, that Penny found it almost pleasurable to introduce herself with her new title. It made the girl's eyes go round for a moment, and then her face fell.

'Your Grace? I believe there has been a misunderstanding. You husband the duke must have been seeking my predecessor in this shop.'

'There is no Madame Giselle, as it says on the door?'

The woman laughed. 'Unfortunately, no. Until her death, she was my employer. She had been in this location for many years.'

'And before she died, you were…'

'A seamstress, your Grace. Madame died suddenly. There was no family to take the shop, and many orders still to fill. It made sense to step out from the back room and become Madame Giselle, in her absence.' The French accent had disappeared to reveal the Londoner underneath. Apparently, she'd taken more than the shop when she'd come out from the back room.

The girl took her silence as hesitation. 'We are not as fashionable as we once were, I'm afraid. I will understand, of course, that you prefer to go elsewhere. I can recommend several excellent modistes who are frequented by the ladies of your class.'

If she was not careful, she'd get her chance to shop with Clarissa. Penny's eyebrows arched in surprise. 'No wonder you are not as busy as you should be. For when one is in trade, one should never turn down commerce, especially an order as large as the one I am likely to make.' When she had come into the shop, she had had no intention of spending money. But suddenly, it seemed the most natural thing in the world.

'A large order?' the dressmaker repeated, dumbly.

'Yes. Day dresses, travelling clothes, outerwear and ball gowns. I need everything.'

'Do you wish to look at swatches?'

She gritted her teeth. 'It does not matter. Choose whatever you wish. And styles as well. I do not have any idea how to proceed.' And then she prepared for the worst.

The girl ran her through her paces, draping her in fabrics, and experimenting with laces and trims. And Penny had to admit that it was not as bad as it could have been, for the girl made no attempt to force her into gowns that did not flatter, but chose clothes that would suit her, rather than poking and pinching to get her to fit the fashion.

The choice of shops had been most fortunate, although Adam could not have known it. Now if she could find a way around the inconvenience of dinner and dancing for a hundred or so of her husband's friends… The man was cracked if he thought he could use his mother's guest lists. The names on it were likely to be as dead as her modiste.

Penny glanced down at the girl, who was crouched at her feet, setting a hem in the peach muslin gown Penny was modelling. 'Giselle?'

'My real name is Sarah, your Grace,' she said, around a mouthful of pins. 'Not as grand as it should be. But there is no point in hiding the truth.'

'Sarah, then. Do you have family in service?'

'My mother is housekeeper at Lord Broxton's house.'

One of her husband's adversaries in Parliament, but closely matched in society. It would do to go on with. 'It seems, Sarah, that I am to throw a ball. But I am no more born to be a duchess than you were born a French-woman. If I had guest lists and menus from a similar party, it would help me immensely. No one need know, of course. And I would be willing to pay, handsomely.'

Jem was summoned from the street and given a note from Sarah, and directions to the Broxtons' kitchen door.

He was back in a little more than an hour, with a tightly folded packet of papers containing names and addresses of the cream of London society, and the menus for a variety of events.

Penny sat comfortably on a stool in the back room and smiled at Sarah, who was throwing a hem into another sample gown. 'This is turning out to be a surprisingly productive trip, and not the total waste of time I had suspected. If I am careful, and can avoid any more of my husband's outlandish plans for me, I might still manage an hour or two of work.'

Adam would no doubt be irate when he saw the clothing that that woman was making for her. It did not in any way remind her of the dresses worn by the ladies of his circle. The colours for evening were pale, and the sprigged muslins she had chosen for day dresses hardly seemed the thing for a duchess.

Although just what duchesses wore during the day, Penny was unsure. Whatever they liked, most likely.

She gritted her teeth again. Or whatever their husband insisted they wear. But Sarah had seemed to know her business, despite the lack of customers. She had loaded Penny up with such things as were ready, more than enough petticoats, bonnets, and a few day dresses that had been made for samples, but fit so well they might have been tailored for her.

She inquired of the total, not daring to imagine how much she might have spent.

She saw the wistful look in the girl's eye as she said, 'The bills will be sent to your husband, of course. You needn't worry about anything, your Grace.'

Of course not. For nobility did not have to concern themselves with a thing so mundane as money. But she had taken much of the poor girl's sample stock, and there would be silks to buy, and lace, and ribbon to complete the order.

And since she was the Duchess of Bellston, it could all be had on credit while the false Madame Giselle found a way to pay her creditors with aristocratic air. Her husband, who had been so eager for this wardrobe, would send the girl some money in his own good time. She must manage as she could until then.

Penny reached into her reticule, and removed a pack of folded bank notes, counting out a thick stack. 'Here, my dear. This should go a fair way in covering the materials you will need. You may send the balance directly to my bank for immediate payment. Do not hesitate to contact me, should you need more. If I must do this at all, I would that it be done right and wish you to spare no expense.'

She saw the visible sag of relief, and the broadening of the smile on the face of the modiste.

When the carriage returned, and Jem saw the pile of boxes, he looked at her with suspicion, and gestured to an underfootman to throw them on to the carriage and tie them down. 'I'm to spend all my time, now that you're a "her Grace" two steps back and carrying your ribbons?'

'If it makes you feel better, Jem, think of it as charity work, just as my brother always wanted me to do. Or perhaps as economic investment in a small business.'

Jem stared sceptically at the boxes. 'I'm thinking, at least ladies' dresses are lighter than books.'

'Well, then. You have nothing to complain about.'

She had chosen to wear one of her new dresses home, a simple thing in pale pink muslin, with a rose-coloured spencer. The matching bonnet was a work of extreme foolishness, with a shirred back and a cascade of ribbons, but it seemed to suit the dress and she did not mind it overmuch. When she walked up the steps to the townhouse, it was a moment before the man at the door recognised her, and smiled before bowing deep.

Very well. The transformation must be startling. Adam would be pleased. She was certain of it. And he would admire the way she had managed the ball with a minimum of effort.

And then she remembered it did not matter at all to her what Adam thought. The whole of this production was an attempt to fool society into believing in their sham marriage, and put up a united front for his spurned lover, Clarissa.

If she was truly spurned. It was quite possible that Penny had wandered on to the scene in the middle of a contretemps and things would be returning to their despicable normal state at any time. If she allowed herself to care too much about her husband's good opinion, she would feel the pain of his indifference when he was through with her.

She hardened her heart, and walked down the hall to her husband's study, pushing open the door without knocking.

He was not alone. Lord Timothy was there as well. They had been deep in discussion over something, but it came to a halt, as she entered. 'I have returned. As Madame Giselle would say, *"C'est fini"*.' The men stared at her as she pulled the bonnet from her head and dropped it on to her husband's desk. She reached into her reticule and removed the papers. 'Here is the list of guests for your ball. Add any names I have missed to the bottom of the list. Dinner will be buffet, but there will be no oysters, because it is too late in the season. You have but to choose a date. You know your social schedule better than I. For my part, I mean to be studying every night, for the foreseeable future. Which means any night you choose for this ball is equally inconvenient.

'Once you have decided, send the cursed guest list to the printer yourself. If you do not know where I wish you to take it, I will tell you, in no uncertain terms.' She looked down her nose at her husband, in what she hoped was a creditable imitation of a *ton* lady. 'Is that satisfactory, your Grace?'

Her husband stared at her in shocked silence. Lord Timothy grinned at her in frank admiration and supplied, 'Oh, yes. I should think so.'

'Very well, then. I shall retire, in my mildly pink dress, to my incredibly pink sitting room, put my feet on a cushion and read Gothic novels. I do not wish to be disturbed.' She turned to cross the hall, only to have Tim bound ahead of her to open the door.

Before it shut behind her, she heard a noise from the study that sounded suspiciously like a growl.

Chapter Twelve

Adam stared through the open door of his study at the closed door across the hall. The silence emanating from the room was like a wall, laid across the threshold to bar his entrance. She spoke to him no more than was necessary, ate in her rooms and politely refused all visitors. She had succeeded in achieving the marital state that they had agreed on, allowing herself total solitude, and deeding complete freedom to him. He could do as he wanted in all things. His life was largely unchanged from the one he had before the marriage, with the exception of a near-unlimited supply of funds.

Why did he find it so vexing?

Perhaps because he had grown tired of that life, and had been quite ready to end it by any means available. Sick to death of playing, by turns, the wit, the lover or the buffoon for a series of false friends. Bone weary of dodging the insistent affections of Clarissa, who refused to believe that he looked back on their affair with regret and self-disgust.

And Tim, still at his side as a true friend and adviser. He chose to play the absentminded academic, more interested in his books and his conservatory than in the people around him. He pretended no knowledge of what had occurred between Adam and his wife, until such moments as he let slip an idle comment or odd turn of phrase to prove he knew exactly what had occurred, and was disappointed, but not particularly surprised.

Adam had hoped that the introduction of Penelope to his life might lead to a lasting change. She had qualities most unlike the other women of his set: sweetness, sincerity and a mind inquisitive for things deeper than the latest fashion. And she had seemed, for a time, to hold him in respect. He must present a much different picture in *The Times* than he did in reality. For though she claimed to respect Bellston, the politician, it had taken her a week to become as disgusted with Bellston, the man, as he was himself.

A servant entered, offering him a calling card on a silver tray.

Hector Winthorpe.

It was some consolation to see that the card was impeccably done, for Adam had sent the invitations for the ball to the Winthorpe shop. And he had grudgingly added Hector's name to the bottom of the guest list, as a good faith gesture. The man would not fit, but what could be done? Hector was family and they must both get used to it. But what the devil was he doing, coming to the house now?

Adam gave his permission to the servant and in a moment, Hector entered the room without making a bow, then stood too close to the desk, making every effort to tower over him.

Adam responded with his most frosty expression and said, 'If you are searching for your sister, she is across the hall. But it is pointless to try, for she refuses visitors when she is at work.'

'You have had no better luck with her than I did, I see, if she is shut up alone in a library. But I did not come for her. I wish to speak to you.'

'State your business, then.'

'It is about this, your Grace.' There was no respect or subservience in the title, as the man slapped the invitation to the ball on the desk in front of him.

'A written response of regrets would have been sufficient.'

'Regrets? It is you, sir, who should have regrets.'

Adam stared back, angry, but curious. 'And what precisely should I regret, Hector? Marrying your sister? For I find I have surprisingly few regrets where she is concerned.'

Hector sniffed in disapproval. 'Because she has given you your way in all things, I suppose. And because you care naught for her happiness, you have no guilt of the fact. If you felt anything at all for her, you would know better than this.'

Adam stared down at the invitation, truly baffled now. 'I fail to see what is so unusual about a small gathering to celebrate our nuptials.'

'Small?' Hector shook his head. 'For you, perhaps.

But for my sister, any gathering over two is a substantial crowd.'

'That is ridiculous. I have noticed no problems.' Which was a lie, but he could not give the man the upper hand so easily.

Hector let out a disgusted snort. 'If you noticed no problems with my sister, it is because she is a proud woman, and does not wish to admit to them. Did you not think it strange that she wanted nothing more from you than a chance to lock herself in her study and read?'

'Not overly,' he lied again, thinking of his first suspicions of her.

'Or that an argument over something so simple as a book would drive her to such extreme action as marrying a total stranger?'

There was nothing he could say that would cover the situation, and he certainly could not tell the whole truth, which reflected badly on the man's sister as well as himself. 'It has not proved a problem thus far.' He turned the argument back upon its sender. 'Do you think she chose unwisely?' And then he waited for the apology that must surely come.

'Yes, I do, if you mean to trot her out before your friends as some sort of vulgar joke.'

'How dare you, sir!'

Hector continued to be unabashed by the situation. 'It was too late, by the time she brought you to our home, to insist that you answer this question. But what are your intentions toward my sister, if not to make her the butt of your jokes?'

Adam smiled bitterly. 'I do not mean to fritter away

her fortune, as you were doing. You were keeping her unmarried and under your control so that you could pour her money into your business.'

The shot hit home, and he saw rage in Hector's eyes. 'I am not proud of the fact that the business is in trouble, sir. And I did, indeed, borrow the money from her trust without inquiring of her first. It was wrong of me, for certain. But I did not need to keep her unmarried to plunder her fortune. She did quite a fine job of scaring away any potential mates when she had her come-out. Her subsequent isolation was all her own doing. As of late, it had become quite out of hand. When I attempted to correct her on this, she lost her temper and went to Scotland. Apparently, she was looking for any fool that would have her. And she found you.' Hector said the word as though his sister had crossed the border and picked up not a husband, but some exotic disease.

Adam refused to rise to the bait. 'She can be rash, of course. But I fail to see what is so serious in her behaviour that would cause you to censure her or deny her simple purchases. It was wrong of you, just as was the theft of her money.'

'What do you know of her social life before you married her?'

Adam tried to think of anything he could say that would make him sound like he was an active participant in his own marriage, who had taken the time to get to know his wife, either before of after the ceremony. At last he said, 'Nothing. Other than her reasons for wishing to marry, and that she was interested in translating the classics, she has told me nothing at all.'

'Did you not think it odd that she has had no visits from friends, congratulating her on her marriage?'

He had not questioned it. But of course, there should have been guests to the house. If it had been any other woman, her friends would have beaten a path to the door, eager to meet the peer and bask in the reflected glow of Penny's rise in stature. 'I thought perhaps she had cast them off as unworthy. Now that she is a duchess…'

He could not manage to finish the sentence. He had thought no such thing. It was impossible to imagine Penny, who had little interest in her title or anyone else's, being capable of such cruelty to her friends.

Hector was silent, letting the truth sink in. And then he confirmed Adam's new suspicions. 'She has received no visitors because there is no one who has missed her. No one has expressed concern at her absence, or will wish her well on her good fortune. She has no friends, sir. None.'

'That is strange.' He could not help but say it, for it was. 'There is nothing about her that would indicate the fact. She does not complain of loneliness. Nor is there any reason that people might shun her society.'

'That is because she has been most effective at shunning the society of others. Her behaviour in public is, at best, outlandish, and at worst disturbing. When Father tried to give her a come-out, she made such a fool of herself that before the Season was complete, she had taken to her bed and was unwilling even to come down for tea. We hoped, with time, she would calm herself. But by the next year she was even more set in her ways than she had been. Small gatherings made her nervous, and large groups left her almost paralysed with fear.'

Hector looked at Adam with suspicion. 'And so it went, until she went off to Scotland in a huff, and came back with you. You will find, once you get to know her, that no fortune will make up for deficiencies of the mind.' His smile twisted with cruelty. 'Or do you claim some sudden deep affection for the girl that caused you to sweep her from her feet?'

Once again, Adam was trapped between the truth and the appearance of the thing. 'I can say in all honesty that I did not know of her fortune when I married her. And as far as my deep and abiding affection for her...' the words stuck in his throat '...you will never hear me claim otherwise, in public or private.'

Hector smiled and nodded. 'Spoken like a politician. It is not a lie, but it tells me nothing of what really happened.'

Adam stared at him without answering.

'Very well.' Hector tapped the invitation on the desk. 'You will not explain. But as a politician, you must be conscious of how her behaviour will reflect on you. It might be best to cut your losses, before she exposes herself, as she is most sure to do, and brings scandal down upon you.'

Adam drew in a breath. 'Cut my losses. And how, exactly, do you propose I do that?'

Hector smiled. 'You may think it is too late to seek an annulment. But you can hardly be expected to remain married, if there is any question as to the mental soundness of one of the parties involved. Think of the children, after all.'

'And if I cast her off?'

'I would take her back, and make sure she had the care she needed.'

When hell freezes. 'And you will take her money as well, I suppose.' Adam made a gesture, as if washing his hands. 'You are right, Winthorpe. I am growing worried about what a child of this union may be like. Suppose my heir should take after you? If that is not reason to remain childless, I cannot think of a better one. And as for any balls or entertainments we might choose to have? Such things are between myself and my wife and none of your affair.' But he felt less confident than he had before.

Hector threw his hands in the air. 'Very well, then. On your head be it if the poor girl drops on the dance floor in a fit of nervous prostration. Do not say you were not warned. The wilfulness of marrying was her doing. But you, sir, must take credit for the damage from now on.' And with that, he collected his hat and left the house.

Adam stared across the hall and felt a wave of protectiveness for the woman behind the closed door. Her brother was even more repellent than Adam had imagined, and he understood why she might have been willing to risk a stranger over another moment with Hector.

His accusation was a ploy to regain control of her fortune, of course. But suppose his wife was as frightened of society as her brother claimed? It explained much of Penny's behaviour, since they had been married. She was obviously happier alone with her books. It would be terribly unfair of him to expect her to stand before his friends as hostess.

Unfair, but necessary. People would talk, of course. There was no stopping it when Clarissa was egging them on. The longer his wife hid behind her studies, the louder the voices would become, and the crueller the speculations. A single evening's entertainment would do much to settle wagging tongues.

But the sight of her, frozen in terror in front of a hundred guests, would do nothing to help and much to hurt. Hector was right in that, at least. He must avoid that, at all costs.

He rose, crossed the hall and knocked upon her door, opening it before she could deny him.

She was seated in a chair at the tiny writing desk in the corner, attired in a pale blue gown that must have been one of the purchases he had forced upon her. He doubted it would win favour to tell her that the colour and style suited her well, although, in truth, they did. She looked quite lovely in the morning sunlight, surrounded by books.

She set down the volume she had been reading, pushed her glasses up her nose and looked up at him with cool uninterest. 'Is there something that I can help you with?'

How best to broach the question? 'I was wondering—are preparations for the ball progressing well?'

She nodded, and he felt the tension in the air as she stiffened. 'As well as can be expected. The invitations have been sent, and replies are returning. The hall is cleaned, the food is ordered.'

'I thought…perhaps we could cancel the plans, if it is being too much trouble.'

She was looking at him as though he had lost his

mind. 'After all the trouble of choosing the food, decorating the hall, and sending the invitations, you now wish me to spend even more time in sending retractions?'

'No. Really, I—'

'Because if you think, at this date, it is possible to stop what you wished to set in progress, you are quite mad.'

He closed his eyes and took a deep breath, vowing to remain calm in the face of her temper, no matter what might occur. 'I do not wish to make more work for you, or to take you from your studies. I swear, that was never my goal. My decision to hold the ball was made in haste, and without any thought to your feelings or needs. It pains me greatly that you heard of it from someone other than myself, for it further displayed my carelessness in not coming to you immediately to explain.'

'Apology accepted.' She turned back to her books, as though to dismiss him.

'Your brother was here. In my study, just now.'

That had her attention. She looked up at him in surprise. 'Whatever did he want?'

'He came to throw my invitation back in my face and tell me that you were unfit to attend such an event, much less be the hostess. And that I was a brute for forcing you into it.'

She laughed with little confidence and no mirth. 'It is a pity I was not there to thank him, his faith in my emotional stability has always meant so much to me.'

'What happened when you had your Season to give him such ideas?'

'It was nothing, really.'

'I do not believe you.'

She shook her head. 'I was a foolish girl…'

He stepped farther into the room, moving toward her without thinking. 'You might have been impetuous. But I cannot imagine you a fool. Tell me the story, and we will never speak of it again.'

'Very well.' She sighed. 'The truth about my come-out—and then you will see what a ninny you have married. I have always been awkward in crowds, more comfortable with books than with people. But my father admired my studiousness and did nothing to encourage me to mix with others my age. It was not until I was seventeen, and he sought to give me a Season, that the problems of this strategy became apparent.'

Adam pulled a chair close to hers, sat down beside her, and nodded encouragingly.

'Mother was long past, and there was little my father or brother could do to help me prepare for my entrance into society. Father engaged a companion for the sake of propriety, but the woman was a fifty-year-old spinster. She knew little of fashion and nothing of the ways of young ladies, other than that they needed to be prevented from them. I was more than a little frightened of her. I suspect she increased the problems, rather than diminishing them.'

She paused and he wondered if she meant to leave the story at that. He said, 'So you had your come-out, and no one offered. Or were you unable to find someone to suit yourself?'

She shook her head. 'Neither is the case, I'm afraid.

Any young girl with a dowry the size of mine could not help but draw interest. Father dispensed with the fortune hunters, and encouraged the rest. And at the end of the summer, there was a young man who seemed to suit. He was a lord of no particular fortune, but he seemed genuine in his affection for me.' She looked up at him, puzzled. 'It was so easy, when I was with him, to behave as the other girls did. The crowds were not so daunting. I grew to look to the parties and balls with anticipation, not dread. And I did quite enjoy the dancing...' Her voice trailed away again.

She had been in love. Adam felt a bolt of longing at the idea that his wife had known happiness, before she had known him.

She came back into the present and smiled at him, bright and false. 'And then I overheard my beloved ex-plaining to a girl I thought a friend that, while he loved this other girl above all things, he would marry me for my money, and that was that.

'A sensible girl might have ignored the fact and con-tinued with what would have been a perfectly accept-able union. Or broken it off quietly and returned to try again the next Season. But not I. I returned to the room and told the couple, and all within earshot, that I thought them as two-faced as Janus for denying their hearts with their actions, and that I would rather die than yoke myself to a man that only pretended to love me for the sake of my money. Then I turned on my heel, left the assembly rooms and refused all further invitations. My mortification at what I had done was beyond bearing. I had not wanted to draw attention to myself. I only hoped to find someone who would want me for who I was. Was it so much to ask? But my brother assured me that I had shamed the family. No one would have me, now I'd made such a cake of myself.' She smiled, wistfully. 'The last thing I should have done, to achieve my ends, was behave in a way that, I'm sorry to say, is very much in my character.'

Adam felt the rage boiling in his heart and wished that he could find the man who had been so callous to her, and give him what he deserved. Then he would pay a visit to her brother, and give Hector a dose of the same.

She swallowed and lifted her chin. 'Of course, you can see that I have learned my lesson. I expected no such foolishness when I married you. If we must hold a ball and make nice in front of your friends, so be it. As long as there is no pretence between us that the event means something more than it truly does.' She lowered her eyes and he thought for a moment he could see tears shining in them, although it might have been the reflection of the afternoon light on her spectacles.

And he reached out spontaneously and seized her hand, squeezing the fingers in his until she looked up at him. 'I would take it all back if I could. Throw the invitations on the fire before they could be sent. You must know that I have no desire to force you into behaviours that will only bring back unpleasant memories. It was never my intention to make you uncomfortable or unhappy. And if there is anything I can do to help…'

Perhaps he sounded too earnest, and she doubted his sincerity. For when she looked at him, her face was blank and guarded. 'Really, Adam. You have done more than enough. Let it be.'

But damn it all, he did not want to let it be. He wanted to fix it. 'The ball will go on. There is no stopping it, I suppose. But in exchange, I will do something for you.'

She was staring at him as though the only thing she wished was that he leave her alone. What could he possibly do? It was not as if he could promise her a trip to the shops. She had made it clear enough what she thought of them, when he had forced her to go the first time. And if her mind had changed and she wished such things, she could afford to purchase them for herself.

And then, the idea struck him. 'At the ball, we will announce that it is our farewell from society, for a time. We will be repairing to our country home. There, you will have all the solitude you could wish for. It is Wales, for heaven's sake. Beautiful country, and the place where my heart resides, but very much out of the way of London society. Your books can be sent on ahead, to greet you in the library when we arrive. Between the house and the grounds, there is so much space that you can go for days without seeing a soul. Dead silence and no company but your books, for as long as you like.'

Her eyes sparkled at the sound of the word 'library'. And she seemed to relax a bit. 'This will be our only party, then?'

'For quite some time. I will make no more rash pronouncements in public without consulting you first.'

'And we may go the very next day?' She seemed far more excited by the prospect of rustication, than she did by the impending ball.

'If you wish it.' He smiled. 'And we will see if you prefer it to London. But I warn you, it is frightfully dull at Felkirk. Nothing to do but sit at home of an evening, reading before the fire.'

She was smiling in earnest now. And at him. 'Nothing to do but read. Really, your Grace. You are doing it far too brown.'

'You would not be so eager if I told you about the holes in the roof. The repairs are not complete, as of yet. But the library is safe and dry,' he assured her. 'And the bedrooms.'

And suddenly, her cheeks turned a shade of pink that, while very fetching, clashed with the silk on the walls. To hide her confusion, she muttered, 'That is good to know. The damage was confined, then, to some unimportant part of the house?'

And it was his turn to feel awkward. 'Actually, it was to the ballroom. When I left, it was quite unusable.'

And her blush dissolved into a fit of suppressed giggles. 'It devastates me to hear it, your Grace.'

'I thought it might. I will leave you to your work, then. But if you need help in the matter of the upcoming event, you will call upon me?'

She smiled again. 'Of course.'

'Because I am just across the hall.' He pointed.

'I know.' She had forgiven him. At least for now. He turned to leave her, and glanced with puzzlement at a lone remaining Meissen figurine, turned face to the wall and occupying valuable space on his wife's bookshelf. He shook his head at the carelessness of the servants, and turned it around, so that it faced properly into the room. 'I will send someone to have this removed, if it annoys you.'

She shook her head. 'Do not bother. I have grown quite used to it.'

Chapter Thirteen

The night of the ball had finally arrived, and Adam hoped that his wife was not too overwrought by the prospect. He had nerves enough for both of them.

Clarissa would be there, of course. He combed his hair with more force than was necessary. Another meeting with her was unavoidable. He could not hold a party and invite his friend, only to exclude his wife. There was very little to do about Clarissa without cutting Tim out of his social circle entirely. And he could hardly do that. They had been friends since childhood. Tim's unfortunate marriage to the shrew, and Adam's regrettable behaviour over her, had done nothing to change it, although Adam almost wished it had. It would have been so much easier had Tim called him out and shamed him in public, or at least cut him dead. But the veneer of civility, when they were together at a social gathering, was a torture much harder to endure.

He hoped that the presence of Penny, and success of the evening, would cool the look in Clarissa's eye.

There was a change in the light that fell upon the table, and a discreet clearing of a throat.

He looked up into the mirror to see his wife standing in the connecting doorway behind him.

He didn't realise he had been holding his breath until he felt it expel from his lungs in a long, slow sigh. It was his wife, most certainly. But transformed. The gown was a pale green, and with her light hair and fair skin, she seemed almost transparent. As she came towards him, he imagined he was seeing a spirit, a ghost that belonged to the house, that had been there long before he had come.

And then the light from his lamp touched the gown and the sarsenet fabric shifted in colour from silver to green again, and the silver sequins sparkled on the drape of netting that fell from her shoulder to the floor.

Even her glasses, which had seemed so inappropriate and unfeminine when he first met her, completed the image as the lenses caught the light and threw it back at him, making her eyes shimmer.

His friends would not call her a beauty, certainly. She was most unlike all the other women who were lauded as such. But suddenly it did not matter what his friends might say. It only mattered what he knew in his heart to be true—she looked as she was meant to look. And now that he had removed her from whatever magic realm she had inhabited, he was overcome with the desire to protect her from the coarse harshness of the world around them.

She had reached his side, and tipped her head quizzically to the side. 'Is it all right?'

He nodded and smiled. 'Very much so. You are lovely.'

'And you are a liar.' But he could see the faint blush on her cheek as she said it.

'You're welcome. It is a most unusual gown. Vaguely Greek, I think, and reminiscent of the Penelope of legend. And therefore, most suitable for you. Are you ready to greet our guests?'

'Yes.' But he saw the look in her eyes.

'And now you are the one who is lying.'

'I am as ready as I am ever likely to be.'

'Not quite. There is something missing. I meant to deal with it earlier, but I quite forgot.'

He removed the jewel box from where he had left it in the drawer of his dresser. 'It seems, in the hurry to marry, that we forgot something. You have no ring.'

'It is hardly necessary.'

'I beg to differ. A marriage is not a marriage without a ring. Although the solicitors and banks did not comment, my friends must have noticed.'

She sighed. 'You do not remember, do you? You gave me a ring, when we were in Gretna. I carry it with me sometimes. For luck.' She pulled a bent horse nail from her fine silk skirts and slipped it on to her finger. 'Although perhaps I need the whole shoe for it to be truly lucky. I do not know.'

He stared down at it in horror. 'Take that from your finger, immediately.'

'I had not planned to wear it, if that is your concern. It is uncomfortably heavy, and hardly practical.'

He held out his hand. 'Give it here, this instant. I will dispose of it.'

She closed her hand possessively over it. 'You will do nothing of the kind.'

'It is dross.' He shook his head. 'No, worse than that. Dross would be better. That is a thing. An object. An abomination.'

'It is a gift,' she responded. 'And, more so, it is mine. You cannot give it me, and then take it back.'

'I had no idea what I was doing. I was too drunk to think clearly. If I had been sober, I would never have allowed you to take it.'

'That is not the point,' she argued. 'It was a symbol. Of our…' She was hunting for the right word to describe what had happened in Scotland. 'Our compact. Our agreement.'

'But I have no desire for my friends to think I would seal a sacrament with a bent nail. Now that we are in London, I can give you the ring that you by rights deserve.'

She sighed. 'It is not necessary.'

'I believe that it is.'

'Very well, then. Let us get on with it.'

Another proof that his wife was unlike any other woman in London. In his experience, a normal woman would have been eager for him to open the jewel case on his desk, and beside herself with rapture as he removed the ring. The band was wide, wrought gold, heavy with sapphires, set round with diamonds. 'Give me your hand.'

She held it out to him, and he slipped it on to her finger.

It looked ridiculous, sitting on her thin white fingers,

as though it had wandered from the hand of another and settled in the only place it felt at home. She flexed her hand.

She shook her head. 'I retract what I said before. In comparison, the horse nail is light. This does not suit.'

'We can go to the jewellers tomorrow, and get it sized to you.'

'You do not understand. It fits well enough, but it does not suit me.'

'It was my mother's,' he said. 'And my grand-mother's before her.'

'Well, perhaps it would suit, if I were your mother,' she snapped. 'But I am your wife. And it does not suit me.'

'You are my wife, but you are also Duchess of Bellston. And the Duchess wears the ring, in the family colours of sapphire and gold.'

'*My* mother was happy with a simple gold band,' she challenged.

'*Your* mother was not a duchess.'

'When your mother worked, did she remove the ring, or leave it on? For I would hate to damage it.'

'Work?'

'Work,' she repeated firmly.

'My mother did not work.'

'But, if you remember our agreement, I do.' She slipped the ring off her finger and handed it back to him. 'My efforts here are hardly strenuous, but a large ring will snag in the papers and could get soiled, should I spill ink. It is not a very practical choice.'

'Practicality has never been an issue,' he admitted.

'It is to me. For I am a very practical person.'

'I am aware of that.'

She looked at the box on the table, which was large enough to hold much more than a single ring. 'Is there not another choice available that might serve as compromise?'

He re-opened the box, and turned it to her. 'This is a selection of such jewellry as is at the London address. I dare say there is more, in the lock rooms at Bellston.'

She rejected the simple gold band she saw as being a trifle too plain for even the most practical of duchesses, and chose a moonstone, set in silver. It was easily the least worthy piece in the box, and he wondered why his mother had owned it, for it was unlike any of her other jewellry. His wife ran the tip of her finger lightly along the stone: a cabochon, undecorated, but also unlikely to get in the way of her work. 'I choose this.'

'Silver.' He said it as though it were inferior, but then, at one time, he might have said the same of her, had he not been forced to recognise her. And he would have been proved wrong.

'At least I will not feel strongly, should I damage it. And for formal engagements, I will wear your mother's ring. But not tonight.' She slipped the moonstone on to her hand, and it glittered eerily.

'It suits you,' he conceded.

'I suspected it would. And it is better, is it not, than if I wore the horse nail?' She admired the ring on her hand and smiled.

He smiled as well. 'I feared, for a moment, that you might do it, out of spite.'

'I am not usually given to act out of spite,' she said.

He laughed.

'Well, perhaps, occasionally.' Then she laughed as well, and surrendered. 'All right. Frequently. But I shall be most co-operative tonight, if you shall take me to Wales tomorrow.'

'A bargain, madam.' He reached out and took her hand. 'Let us climb the stairs and await our guests.'

Whoever had selected the top floor of the house for a ballroom had not made the most practical of choices, but Adam had to admit that the tall windows, front and back, provided a splendid view of London below, and the night sky above. He felt Penny tense as the first guests arrived, and thought to offer her a last chance to return to her room and avoid the evening. But he saw the determined look in her eyes and thought better of it. She meant to hang on, no matter what, although the bows and curtsies of the guests and polite murmurs of 'your Grace' were obviously making her uncomfortable.

He reached out and laid a hand on her back, hoping to convey some of his strength to her. She was able to suppress the brief flinch of surprise he could feel, when his fingers touched the bare skin above her gown. And then he felt her slowly relaxing back against his hand, and step ever so slightly closer to him, letting him support and protect her.

He smiled, because it felt good to know that, whatever else she might feel, she trusted him. And it felt good as well, to feel her skin beneath his hand. He shifted and his hand slid along her back, and it was smooth and cool and wonderful to touch. The flesh warmed beneath his hand as the blood flowed to it.

And he found himself wondering, would the rest of her feel the same? If he allowed his fingers to slip under the neckline of her gown, would she pull away in shock, or move closer to him, allowing him to take even greater liberties?

'Adam? Adam?'

He came back to himself to find his wife staring up at him in confusion. Her eyes shifted slightly, to indicate the presence of guests.

'Tim and Clarissa, so good to see you.' He smiled a welcome to his friend and nodded to the woman beside him. 'Forgive me. My mind was elsewhere.' He could feel Penny's nervousness under his hand and drew her closer to him.

And as the introductions droned on, his mind returned to where it had been. It might have been easier to concentrate, if he did not have the brief memory of her, changing clothes in his bed. She had been very like a surprised nymph in some classic painting. Beautiful in her nakedness, and unaware of the gaze of another. And he had allowed himself to watch her, for even though she was his wife, he had not expected to see that particular sight again.

And now, of all times, he could not get the picture from his head. While the object of the evening was to prove to his social circle that he admired and respected his new wife, it would not do to be panting after her like a lovesick dog. A few dances, a glass of champagne, and he would retire to the card room, to steady his mind with whisky and the dull conversation of his male friends.

* * *

It was going well, she reminded herself, over and over again. She had survived the receiving line, and, except for a moment where Adam behaved quite strangely, it had been without incident. Clarissa had been quite incensed that Adam had not paid her a compliment. But he had barely seemed to notice the woman. It gave her hope that perhaps the worst was over, and that she need see no more of Clarissa after tonight.

She looked around her, at the throng of people enjoying the refreshments, and at the simple buffet, which was anything but. There was enough food for an army, if an army wished to subsist on lobster, ice-cream sculptures and liberal amounts of champagne. The orchestra was tuning, and soon dancing would begin.

Adam was surveying the room from her side. 'You have done well.'

'Thank you.'

He hesitated. 'I understand that this was difficult for you.'

'It was not so bad,' she lied.

He smiled sympathetically and whispered, 'It will be over soon, in any case. The sooner we begin the dancing, the sooner they will leave.'

'We must dance?' What fresh hell was this?

'Of course. It is our ball. If we do not dance, they will not.'

'Oh.' She had been so convinced that she would embarrass herself with the preparations for the party, or disgrace herself in the receiving line, that she had forgotten there would be other opportunities for error.

He took her hand in his and put his other hand to her waist. 'I know it goes against your nature,' he said. 'But let me lead.'

She remembered not to jump as he touched her, for it would be even more embarrassing to demonstrate again that she was not familiar with the feel of his hands on her body. He seemed unperturbed as he led her out on to the floor. 'You have nothing to fear, you know. Even if you stumble, no one will dare comment. I certainly shall not.'

She nodded, to reassure herself.

'Have you waltzed before?'

She could only manage a frantic glance up into his face.

'It does not matter. The music is lovely, and the step is easy to learn. Relax and enjoy it. One two three, one two three. See. It is not a difficult.'

He was right. It was simple enough, when one had so commanding a partner. In this, at least, she could trust him to lead her right, and so she yielded. And he turned her around the dance floor, smiling as though he enjoyed it.

She tried to match his expression. Perhaps that was the trick of it. She had but to act like she was having a pleasant evening, and people would trouble her no further.

'You are a very good dancer,' he remarked. 'Although not much of a conversationalist. I cannot keep you quiet when we are alone together. Why will you not speak now?'

'All these people…' she whispered helplessly.

'Our guests,' he answered.

'Your guests, perhaps, but they are strangers to me.'

'You met them all in the receiving line just now. And yet they frighten you?'

She managed the barest nod.

He laughed, but squeezed her hand. 'You are quite fearless in your dealings with me. Perhaps it will help you to remember that I am the most important person here.'

'And the most modest.' She could not help herself.

He laughed again, ignoring the gibe. 'At any rate, they all must yield to me. And since I intend to yield to you, you have nothing to be afraid of.'

'You yield to me?'

'If you wish, we will cancel the evening's entertainment, and I will send the guests home immediately.'

'For the last time: no. It would be even more embarrassing to do that than to stand in front of them as I do now, looking like a goose.'

He nodded. 'At least you are speaking to me again. Even if you are lying. Your obedient silence just now was most disconcerting. And you do not look like a goose. Do not concern yourself.'

'We are the centre of attention.'

He glanced around. 'So we are. But it cannot be very interesting for them, to stare at us and do nothing. Soon they will find other diversions. See? The floor is beginning to fill with couples. And others are returning to the buffet. Crisis averted. They no longer care about us. As long as the music is good and the wine holds out, they will entertain themselves and we are free to enjoy ourselves for the rest of the evening in peace.'

It was true. The worst was over. She could pretend that she was a guest at her own party, if she wished, and allow the servants to handle the details.

And as he spun her around the room, she relaxed at the sight of smiling faces and happy people.

And there was Clarissa, staring at her with death in her eyes.

He turned her away, so that she could no longer see, and they were on the other side of the room by the time the music stopped. When they parted, he brought her hand to his lips, and she could feel the look of pleasure on her face when he'd kissed the knuckles. And then he turned to part from her.

'You are leaving me alone?' She could not hide the panic in her voice.

He nodded. 'Our job as host and hostess is to entertain the guests, not each other. There is nothing to be afraid of, I assure you. Continue to smile, nod and say "thank you for coming". Much of your work is done.' He smiled again. 'And I swear, once you have done this thing for me, I am yours to command.'

She squared her shoulders and lifted her chin, prepared to meet the horde that had infested her home.

He nodded. 'Very good. If you need me, I will be in the card room, hiding with the other married men. Madam, the room is yours.'

She fought the feeling of disorientation as she watched him go, as if she was being spun by the elements, with no safe place to stand. But she admired the way her husband moved easily through the crowd, stopping to chat as he made his way to the door. Smiling and nodding. Listening more than he spoke. He was an excellent example to her.

What had she to fear from her guests? It was not as it had been, during her come-out, when all the women were in competition, and the men were prizes. The race was over. And, without trying, she had won first place.

She thought how miserable she had been at those balls, and how awkward, and how good it had felt to find a friendly face or hear a hostess's word of welcome or encouragement.

And then she scanned the crowd. There was the daughter of an earl, barely sixteen, excited by her first invitation, but terrified that it was not going well.

Penny made her way to the girl's side. 'Are you enjoying your evening?'

The conversation was unlike anything she'd ever experienced. The girl was in awe of her. The conversation was peppered with so many 'your Grace's' and curtsies, that Penny had to resist the urge to assure the girl that it was not necessary. She was a nobody who had stumbled into a title.

She smiled to herself. The less said on that subject, the better. She had the ear of the most important man in the room. She could do as she pleased. And it pleased her that people like the girl in front of her should be happy. They talked a bit, before she gently encouraged the girl to a group of young people near to her age, and made a few simple introductions. When she left, the girl was on her way to the dance floor with a young man who seemed quite smitten.

After her initial success, Penny threw herself into the

role of hostess as though she were playing a chess game, with her guests as the pieces. Penelope Winthorpe had been an excellent player, and loved the sense of control she got when moving her army around the board. This was no different. Tonight she could move actual knights, and the ladies accompanying them, urging weaker pieces to the positions that most benefited them. While her husband was able to engage people more closely, she enjoyed the gambits she could arrange in a detached fashion. It made for a harmonious whole.

Perhaps that had been her problem all along. She had never been a successful guest. But that did not mean she could not be a hostess.

'Your Grace, may I have a dance?'

She turned, surprised to see her brother-in-law. 'Of course, Will.' She stammered on the familiarity, and felt her confidence begin to fade.

He smiled, and she searched his face for some shred of duplicity or contempt. 'Penelope?' He gestured to the floor. Since she was rooted to the spot, he took her hand, leading her to the head of the set.

She watched him as they danced, comparing him to his older brother. He was not unattractive, certainly, and moved with grace and confidence. But he lacked his brother's easy sense of command. When they reached the bottom of the set and had to stand out, he leaned closer and spoke into her ear. 'I owe you an apology.'

She looked at him without speaking.

'When I found that my brother had married in haste, I told him to get an annulment. I was convinced that you would both regret the decision.'

'I had no idea,' she replied blandly.

He smiled. 'I suspected you had, for I saw the look in your eyes when you left us that night. I am sorry I caused you pain. Or that I meddled in something that was none of my affair to begin with. It is just that...' he shook his head '...Adam has always had an excellent head for politics, and I cannot fault him for his dedication to responsibilities as Bellston. But in his personal life, he has always been somewhat reckless. He thinks last of what would be best for himself in the distant future, and seems to see only what is directly in front of him.'

She shrugged. 'I cannot fault him for that. I, too, have been known to act in haste.'

'Well, perhaps your tendencies have cancelled each other. You appear to be a most successful match.'

She looked sharply at her new brother. 'We do?'

'You are just what my brother needs: a stable source of good advice. He speaks well of you, and he appears happier than I have seen him in a long time.'

'He does?' She tried to hide her surprise.

'Indeed. He is at peace. Not something I am accustomed to seeing, in one so full of motion as Adam is. But his activity in society brings him near to people that are not as good as they could be. Compared to the foolish women that normally flock to his side, you are a great relief to a worried brother. And I can assure you, and your family, if they are concerned, that in my brother you have found a loyal protector and a true friend. I am glad of your union, and wish you well in it.'

'Thank you. That is good to know.' Impulsively, she

reached out and clasped Will's hand, and he returned the grip with a smile.

Her eyes sought her husband on the other side of the room, and she smiled at him as well.

He returned a look that indicated none of the affection that Will had described. Perhaps her new brother was mistaken.

The music ended. 'I will leave you to your other guests, then. I suspect we will have ample time in the future to speak.' And Will took his leave of her.

Another guest asked her to dance. And then another. At last she excused herself from the floor to check on the refreshments. And found Clarissa, standing in her way.

'Penelope, darling. What a charming party.'

There was no way to cut the woman, no matter how much she deserved it. Penny pasted a false smile on her face and responded, 'Thank you,' then went to step around her.

Clarissa reached out to her, in what no doubt appeared to the room as a sisterly gesture of warmth, catching both hands in hers. Then she pulled her close, to whisper what would look to observers like a girlish confidence. 'But if you think it makes any difference to your standing in society, you are wrong.'

Penny summoned her newfound bravery. 'My position in society is secure. I am Duchess of Bellston.'

'In name, perhaps. But in reality, you are a trumped-up shop girl. People know the truth, and they can talk of little else this evening.'

She had heard nothing, and she had been to every corner of the room. It must be a lie, intended to wound her.

But there was no way to be sure.

Then she thought of what Will had said, and tossed her head in her best imitation of someone who did not give a jot for what people 'said'. 'Let them talk, then. They are most unaccountably rude to be doing so in my home while drinking my wine and eating my food.'

'They are saying nothing more than what your husband has said.'

It was her worst fear, was it not? That he felt she was beneath him. And she feared it because it was based in truth. Clarissa must have guessed as much or she would not speak so.

But there was nothing she could do about it now. So she favoured Clarissa with her coldest look, and said nothing.

'He is taking you to Wales, is he? Very good. I heartily approve. You must go home and complete your work which is, no doubt, noble and of much scholarly import.' The last words were sarcastic, as though Penny's life goal was so much nonsense.

'But no matter what you mean to do, I doubt that Adam means to stay with you in isolation, if there are other more entertaining opportunities open to him. He will come back to London, or find a reason to go to Bath, or somewhere else.

'And the minute he does, you will know that he is coming to me. He was happy enough before you arrived on the scene. And he is even happier, now that he has your money. He has told us as much. He simply needs to get you out of the way, so that he may spend it in peace.'

Penny controlled the flinch, for the last words struck as hard as any blow.

Clarissa continued, 'Adam is happy. And I am happy with Adam. You have promised to be happy with your books. You have nothing further to add to the discussion, other than regular infusions of gold.'

Penny struggled to speak. 'And is Timothy happy?'

'Timothy?' Clarissa laughed again.

'Yes. Timothy. Your husband.'

'He is glad to see Adam back, for they are great friends.'

'And it must be very handy for you to share such affection for Adam. They are good comrades, are they not? And if you seek to be unfaithful, how handy that it be with your husband's best friend.'

Clarissa was unaffected. 'Why, yes. It is most convenient.'

'Until you get caught at it. And then there will be the devil to pay, Clarissa. The scandal will be enormous.'

'Caught? Caught by whom exactly? Dear me, Penelope. You make it sound as though we are likely to be run down with a pack of hounds. How diverting.'

'Your husband,' Penelope hissed. 'You must be mad to think that you can carry on in front of him and remain undiscovered. And if you believe, for one minute, that I will allow you to drag my name, and the name of my husband, through the muck with this public display, you are even more mad. This is my first and final warning to you, Clarissa. Stay away from Adam. Or I will tell Timothy what is going on, and he will put an end to it.'

Clarissa laughed, and it was no delicate silvery peal

of ladylike mirth, but a belly-deep whoop of joy. 'You mean to tell my husband? About me and Adam? Oh, my dear. My sweet, young innocent. You do not understand at all, do you? My husband already knows.'

Penny felt her stomach drop and thought with horror that she was likely to be sick on the floor of her own ballroom. What a ludicrous scene that would be. Clarissa, or any of the other ladies of her husband's acquaintance, would have managed a genteel faint.

'Clarissa, we must dance. You have monopolised our hostess long enough.' Lord Timothy was standing behind her, and she prayed that he had not heard what his wife had been murmuring, for the situation was quite mortifying enough.

'But I was having such a lovely chat with Penny.' Clarissa's voice was honey sweet.

'I can see that.' Tim's was ice and steel. 'She bears the look of one who has experienced one of your chats, darling. Drained of blood, and faint of heart. Remove your claws from her and accompany me.' He laid a hand on Clarissa's wrist and squeezed. 'Or I will pry them loose for you.'

Clarissa laughed and released her, then turned to the dance floor. 'Very well, Timothy. Let us dance. So long as it is not a waltz. I am saving the waltzes for someone special.' Then she walked away as though nothing had happened.

Penny stood frozen in place, watching her, and felt Tim's hand upon her shoulder. 'Are you all right?' His face was so close to her that his cheek brushed her hair.

'I will see to it that my wife goes home early. And then we will speak. Until then, do not trouble yourself.'

She nodded without speaking.

He eased away from her, passing by to follow his wife. In a tone loud enough to be heard by people passing, he said, 'Lovely party, your Grace. I never fail to find entertainment on a visit to Bellston.'

Chapter Fourteen

Penny closed her eyes, and focused on the sound of the room, rather than the faces of the people in it. She had thought things were going so well. But now, it was impossible to tell friends from enemies. When she was seventeen, the falsehoods and sly derision had come as a surprise. But she knew better now. When she looked closely at those around her, she could see from the strained expressions on the faces of her husband's friends that she did not fit in.

And the looks of suspicion, jealousy and disdain seemed to follow, wherever Clarissa had been. The woman could spread discord like a bee spreads pollen.

Damn them all. She would send the guests away, just as Adam had told her she could. And never, ever, would she submit to such torture again. In time, Adam would forget about her, since it was obvious that he wished to be elsewhere. If it mattered so much to him that there be entertainment in his house, he would have been at her side when she was all but attacked by his mistress.

She steadied her breathing. To call a sudden halt to the proceedings would be even more embarrassing than to continue with them. If there were any left in the room that were not talking about her, they soon would be, once she drove them from her house and slammed the doors.

She would retire herself, then. It was embarrassing for a hostess to abandon her guests. But she found herself—suddenly indisposed. Too ill to continue, no doubt due to the stress of the event. People would understand. Some would know the cause of the indisposition, but not all. She might still save some small portion of pride.

She had but to find her husband, and tell him that it behoved him, as host, to rise from the card table, and attend to his guests, for she could not hold up another instant.

She exited the hall and was almost in the card room before she knew what she was about. The sound of male laughter echoed into the hallway.

It would be embarrassing to invade the privacy of the men, but it could not be helped. It was her house, after all. Even if she might need to continually remind herself of the fact.

She paused in front of the partially open door, standing behind it, and taking in a deep breath, scented with the tobacco smoke escaping from the room. And without intending to, she heard the conversation, escaping from the room as well.

'Of course, now that Adam is an old married man, he will not be interested in cards or horses. I dare say your new bride does not approve of your track losses, Bellston.'

There was general laughter.

'She has not yet had the chance to approve or disapprove of them, Mark. We have been married a short time, and even I cannot lose money so fast as that, despite my dashed bad luck. When one is throwing one's money away, it takes time to pick a horse that can do the job properly.'

'You took little enough care in the finding of a wife, Adam.'

So she was no different than choosing a jade. Anger mingled with shame at the hearing of it.

'Indeed. You were alone when you left London. Wherever did you find her?' It was her husband's friend, John.

'She found me, more like. I was not even looking.' Her husband's voice.

She drew back from the door. Her father had often told her that people who listened at keyholes deserved what they heard. She should retreat immediately if she did not want Clarissa's stories confirmed.

'She must have a fat purse, then, for you to marry so quickly.'

She could feel her cheeks reddening. *One, two, three…*

'Her father was a cit?' Another voice, edged with curiosity.

Four, five, six.

'In printing, I believe,' her husband answered. 'Books and such. My wife is a great reader. Probably through his influence.'

Someone laughed. 'What does a woman need with reading?'

Idiot. Her fists balled.

'I wouldn't know, myself. But she seems to value it.' There was the faintest trace of sarcasm in her husband's voice. And she relaxed her fists. 'I imagine it proves useful, if one does not wish to appear as foolish as you.'

'But it must take her time away from other, more important things,' John responded. 'Her appearance, for example. She is a bit of a quiz.'

Her husband, and his damned friends, sniping and backbiting, as she had seen them on the first day. She would not cry, she reminded herself. She was a grown woman, in her own house, and she would suffer these fools no longer, but go into the room and remind her husband who had paid for the party.

And then she noticed the silence emanating from the room. John's comment had been followed by a mutter of assent, and some nervous laughter, that had faded quickly to nothing.

Her husband spoke. 'I find her appearance to be singular. Her eyes, especially, are most compelling. Not to everyone's taste, perhaps, but very much to mine. You might wish to remember that, in future, if you wish to visit my home.' The warning in his voice was clear, and she imagined him the way he had been when he stood up to her brother. Quiet, but quite frightening.

Her jaw dropped.

There was more muttering in the room, and a hurried apology from John.

Her husband spoke again. 'If any are curious on the matter of how I came to be married so quickly after my recent financial misfortunes, and to one so wealthy as my wife, let me clarify the situation, that you may explain it to them. It was a chance meeting of kindred souls. The decision on both our parts was very sudden, and on my part, it had very little to do with the size of her inheritance. I consider myself most fortunate to have found so intelligent and understanding a woman, and must regret that circumstances imply an ulterior motive. Would anyone else care to comment on it?'

There were hurried denials from his friends.

'I thought not. Furthermore, I do not expect to hear more on the subject of my wife's family. Her brother is in trade, and our backgrounds are most different. But I wished the woman I married to be worthy of the title, and with sufficient character to bring pride to my name. I am more than happy with my choice. Would that you are all as lucky as I have been.'

Nervous silence followed, and someone cleared his throat.

Then, when tension had reached a near-unbearable point, she heard the sound of shuffling cards, and her husband drawled, 'Another hand, gentleman?'

She could feel the tension release, as the men rushed to offer assent.

She leaned her back to the wall, and let the plaster support her as the room began to spin. The Duke of Bellston found her 'singular'. Whatever did that mean? If another had said it, she'd have thought it was faint praise, and that the speaker had been too kind to say 'odd'.

But from Adam's lips? It had sounded like 'rare'. As though she was something to be sought for and kept safe.

She could not help the ridiculous glow she felt at the knowledge. The most important man in the room thought she did credit to his name. And there had been no false note when he had said he was happy.

She walked slowly down the short hall, toward the ballroom. At the doorway, the butler came to her with a question about the wine, and she answered absently, but with confidence. She could not help smiling, as she went back to her guests, and even managed to stand up for another dance when her husband's brother offered.

The evening was drawing to a close, the crowd already thinning, and it did not really matter if the guests liked her or not. They were leaving soon, and she would be alone with a man who, she smiled to herself, thought she was 'singular'. She looked up to see her husband returning to the main room to seek her out. He took her hand to lead her to the floor for a final dance, but paused, with his head tipped to the side, staring at her.

'Your Grace?' she responded, and smiled back at him.

He shook his head. 'Something is different. What has occurred?'

'I do not know what you mean.'

'You have changed.'

She glanced down at her gown, spreading the skirt with her hand, and shrugged back at him. 'I assure you, I am no different than when we left our rooms earlier today.'

He smiled. 'Perhaps I should have chosen my words more carefully. You are transfigured. I was gone from the room for a short time, and I return to find I've missed a metamorphosis.'

She laughed then, and looked away, remembering his words from earlier. And she could feel the heat in her cheeks as she answered, 'Is this transfiguration a good thing? For not all of them are, you know.'

'I hope so. For you are looking most…well… hmm… I assume you had a pleasant evening.'

'Well enough. But better, now that it is over.' She saw Lord Timothy, staring significantly at her, from across the room. 'If you will excuse me. I think your friend wishes to speak to me.'

'Very well.'

Adam watched her back as she walked away from him and toward the stairs. There was definitely something different about her. A sway in her hips, perhaps? Or a toss of her head as she turned. And her colouring was better. Where she had been deathly pale at the beginning of the evening, to the extent that he feared she might faint in his arms, now there were roses in her cheeks, and a sparkle in her eye. She was smiling as she walked away from him, and he heard her laugh in response to something that Tim had said to her.

The whole impression was most fetching, if a bit disconcerting. As he looked at her, he found himself comparing her with the few ladies remaining in the room. He found the others wanting. She would never be known as a great beauty, but she was certainly handsome. Tonight, she was displaying a strength of character and a confidence that had been lacking in the early days of their marriage. She glanced back at him from her spot beside Tim, and her smile was spontaneous and infectious.

And he had got the distinct impression, when she'd greeted him just now, that she had been flirting with him.

He scanned what was left of the crowd to see if any had noticed, or if there might be some explanation for the change in behaviour. His eye caught his brother, and he signalled him with a nod of his head.

Will crossed the room to his side, smiling and relaxed. It appeared he had also enjoyed the party. 'The evening went well.'

'That is good to know.' Adam indicated his retreating wife with an inclination of his head. 'Penelope did well, I think.'

Will smiled after her. 'So it seems. She is looking most fine this evening.'

Adam nodded agreement. 'What put such colour in her cheeks, I wonder? I spent much of the evening in the card room, and too little time with her.' That his absence might have contributed to her good mood was more than a little irritating.

'Perhaps it was the dancing. I had opportunity to stand up with her on several occasions. She is most adept for one who spends so much time amongst her books. And an intelligent conversationalist, once she overcomes her shyness. It was why I was so opposed to your match. You are a gad, not much for sitting home of an evening, while she would like nothing better. It is not the recipe for a happy union, when two partners are so dissimilar.'

'As you know, with your vast experience as a married man.'

His brother ignored the gibe. 'But I rescind my former feelings on the subject. She seems to be warming to her job as hostess. And once she began to open up to me, I found her views on scholarship to be most refreshing.'

'She opened up to you.'

'Yes. As the evening wore on, she was most chatty. We had several opportunities to speak, as we danced.'

'Oh.' He remembered seeing her, clasping his brother's hand, and the look she had given him, as though she wished him to see. Did she mean to make him jealous? She had succeeded.

Will continued. 'It is good that you plan to allow her to continue with her work. She is correct: her views have value. I most look forward to reading her translation when she completes it.'

Adam searched his heart for a desire to read Homer, in any form, and found it wanting. He could still remember the sting of the ruler on the back of his hand, for all the times he had neglected his studies to go riding, or attempted them, only to miss a conjugation. And now, Will would be there to appreciate the work, once Penny had completed it.

Damn him. But that was ridiculous. He had nothing to fear from his brother. Will would rather die than come between him and his new wife. He should be happy that Penny would have someone to talk to.

Then why did he feel so irritated that she was talking to him tonight? Adam had left her alone to fend for herself. And she had done it, admirably. By the end of the evening, he'd heard murmurs about what a fine hostess she had been, and the people wishing him well had sounded sincere and not sarcastic. The evening had been a success.

And now, his brother could not stop prattling on about his wife's finer qualities, as though they were any business of his. '…and a lot in common with Tim as well. Perhaps when you go home, she will have opportunity to see his research, for I think she would find it fascinating. He was a dab hand at languages when you were in school, was he not?'

'Tim.' *Oh, dear God. Not him as well.*

'Yes. They went off together, just now, while we were speaking? Probably looking for a quiet corner where they can conjugate verbs together.' Will laughed.

'Not if I can help it.' And Adam left his brother to search out his wife.

Chapter Fifteen

'Fair Penelope.' Lord Timothy was being most effusive in his praise, and she wondered if he were the worse for drink. 'I have sent my wife home, and she will bother you no further.'

'You wished to speak to me?'

He caught her hand, and slipped it through the crook of his arm, then led her away from the ballroom. 'In your sitting room, if that is all right. Somewhere we can be alone.'

'What do you wish to say that requires privacy?'

'Things I do not wish others to hear.' He led her past her husband, who was deep in conversation with his brother, and hardly aware of his surroundings. 'Perhaps I wish to be the first man of the *ton* to attempt a flirtation with you. I expect there shall be many, and do not wish to lose my chance, for lack of courage.'

She tried a laugh, and failed. 'If that was meant as a joke, I fear it was not very funny. I do not wish you to flirt with me, now or ever, if that is truly your intent.'

'A pity.' He sighed. 'We would likely do well together, just as our spouses suit each other. For we are studious and bookish, and not at ease in society. Just as they are mercurial and charismatic.'

'It was true what she said, then. You know about them.' Then Penny stopped to look around, afraid that a guest might have heard her speak.

Tim hurried down the last flight of steps and pulled her down the hall and into her own room, shutting the door behind them. 'I am many things, Penelope, but I am neither blind, nor foolish. I was well aware of what happened. Clarissa made certain of it.'

'It does not bother you that your wife is so flagrant in her attentions to other men?'

He sighed. 'Many of the couples in my set have such agreements. We married for reasons other than love. She was rich, as well as beautiful. I have been able to finance my studies.' He grimaced. 'Although she makes me pay dearly for them.'

'And you all look politely the other way when there is something you do not wish to see?'

'Precisely.'

'But if I make the slightest social *faux pas*?'

'Then you will be the talk of the town. You are already notorious for aspiring to a better class than you were born to. People like Clarissa wish to see you fail, to prove that you do not belong. Then they may continue to feel superior.'

'Timothy, this is grossly unfair.'

He nodded. 'But do not believe what she told you. You did well tonight.'

She ignored the compliment. 'It is not particularly moral of you all to allow such chaos and infidelity in your midst.'

'You must have a very limited understanding of society to think so, my dear.'

'I never claimed to have one. Not your idea of society, at least. In the circles I moved in, people did not work so at playing false. My mother loved my father, and my father loved her. They were a most happy couple, until she died. And I would swear they were faithful; even after she was gone, my father did not seek the company of women, or wish to remarry. He threw himself wholeheartedly into his work.'

Timothy laughed. 'Perhaps that is the problem, for we have no work to throw ourselves into. Idle hands, as they say, my dear. Clarissa is proof of that, for she has never done a moment's real labour, but is the devil's handmaiden if there is mischief to be made.'

Penny did not wish to speak ill of the man's wife, and attempted, 'I am sure that she has many qualities that I will consider admirable, once I know her better.'

'And I came here to warn you not to bother. You will never get from her other than you got tonight. Backbiting, sly innuendoes, threats and tricks. If you show weakness, she will use it against you. Once she finds a chink in your armour, she will strike there, to bring you all the pain she can. That is the only reason that she wants Adam back, now that he has finally come to his senses. It amuses her to drive a wedge between me and my oldest friend.'

Penny seized on the only hopeful note in the speech. 'So they are no longer together?'

'Not for some time. But she is persistent, and I feared he would weaken. When he returned from Scotland with you, I was much relieved.'

Penny shook her head. 'It is no love match. Do not expect him to choose me, should there be a choice to be made.'

'And yet, he says he did not marry for money, and I believe him.'

She weighed the truth, and the burden of keeping the secret from one who could help her understand. At last she said, 'We are married because I tricked him. I needed a husband to gain control of my fortune. When I found him, he was face down in a coach yard. It appeared he had tried to throw himself beneath the carriage and make an end of it. He said something about gambling and bad debts when he was sober enough to talk. But he was far too drunk to know what was happening at the time of the actual marriage.'

'It was not binding, if he was too drunk to agree.'

'That was what I thought. I offered to let him go. But he felt an obligation. I needed a husband, and he needed money. And since we were already married, we struck a bargain and came back to London.' She looked sadly at Timothy. 'I am sorry to disappoint you, if you were expecting a grand romantic tale. But that's the truth of it.'

'Nonsense. He is yours if you want him, and Clarissa has no hope. I know him better than I know myself. And I have seen the way he looks at you.'

She laughed. 'What way is that?'

'Like a man in love. You are good for him, Penelope. No matter how things appear, you must not lose heart, for Clarissa is no threat to you.' Tim caught her hand and held it in his.

She laughed. 'You are mad.'

'Adam may be too big a fool to tell you, just yet. But not so big a fool as to pass you by for that harridan I am shackled to. What happened pains him greatly, and I am sick to death of seeing the guilt in his eyes when he looks at me. Make him forget, and you will help us both.'

'But why do you bother, Tim? I am sure he would not blame you if you could not forgive him.'

Tim smiled. 'I know how much of the blame lies with my wife. Clare angled after him for years before she finally trapped him. It was a wonder he held out as long as he did.'

'But she was not the only one at fault,' Penny said.

'True enough. And try as I might, I cannot help but forgive him. I'm sure you have noticed by now that he is a most likeable fellow, especially when you wish to be angry with him. Very persuasive. Has he told you what happened, to get him sent down when we were at school together?'

'No.' She tried to hide her curiosity.

'It was all my doing.' Tim shook his head. 'I was a heavy drinker in those days. And one night, while deep in my cups, we got to brawling with each other in a public house, like common ruffians. That was over a woman as well, for it is the only reason we ever argue. Missed curfew. And gave him the worst of it. Blacked his eye and nearly broke that handsome face of his. It was all around the school that I assaulted Bellston's heir. Added to my lack of academic attention, I deserved a one-way ticket home. But somehow, Adam managed to convince the deans that it was all his fault. Took the whole blame. Issued the apologies, paid the bills, put some ice on his black eyes and allowed himself to be sent home in disgrace to face his father. Told me, if I loved science so much, I had best get about proving it, for with no title and no money, I would need an education to secure my future. But since he was to be duke, he could be as big a fool as he liked and no harm would come of it.'

Tim smiled and shook his head. 'Couldn't well be angry with him after that. You will see what he is like, if you haven't already. When he tries, let him charm you. You will not regret it, I promise you.'

There was a rather loud sound of someone clearing his throat in the hallway, and then the door opened and her husband walked into the room.

Adam glanced at them, as though not noticing anything unusual, and said, 'I was looking for a book, for the trip tomorrow.' He looked at her. 'Perhaps you could recommend something?' And to his friend, 'Or you, Tim. For I assume that is why you are secluded with my wife. So that you may talk books, without boring the rest of us.' There was a touch of menace in her husband's voice that she had never heard before.

'Of course,' Tim answered innocently. 'For what other reason would one choose to be alone with such a lovely woman? Not making you jealous, am I?'

'Do I have reason to be?'

'I think I might have reason to be jealous of you. But that is between you and your wife. Good luck, old friend, as if you need any more. And goodnight.' Tim let go of her hand, and rose to leave.

Adam watched him with suspicion. 'Close the door behind you, please.'

He waited until his friend had gone down the hall and was out of earshot. And then he said without warning, 'I will not let you cuckold me in my own home.'

'Would you prefer that I do it elsewhere?' She had almost laughed at the ridiculousness of it before she realised he was serious.

He did not raise his voice, but she could tell that his temper was barely contained. 'You know what I meant. I would prefer not to have to kill a man over you. Especially not that one.'

'Kill Tim? Adam, listen to yourself. Have you gone mad?'

She could hardly recognise the man before her, for his eyes were dark and his face more grim than she had ever seen it. 'Do not be flip with me. If you do not set that young puppy straight, I will be forced to deal with him on the field of honour, the next time I wander in on the two of you.'

'For holding my hand? That is rich, after what he has suffered from you.'

'Which is another reason I do not wish to hurt him. He has not, as yet, done anything I cannot overlook. But I suspect it is only a matter of time before I will have reason to act. I beg you to stop it, to prevent me from having to do so.'

She rolled her eyes. 'As if it would matter to you. From what I gather, in talking to your friends, the nobles of your acquaintance have the morals of cats in an alley. Not one wife amongst them is faithful, and all the husbands have mistresses.'

'That is different,' he answered.

'I fail to see how. It is not as if we married for love, unless that is a mandatory precursor to the level of infidelity I have seen. Ours was a purely financial arrangement, and I thought we were of an understanding on the subject of sexual attachments. I told you it did not matter to me.'

'And do you remember my saying, in response to you, that what you did would not matter to me? Because I did not. I was under the impression that while you intended for me to find a mistress to deal with my personal needs, you meant to stay home alone with a good book.'

'So the situation is agreeable, so long as it benefits you and not me?' she said.

'I fail to see how it does, since I have not yet taken advantage of the liberties you seem so eager to allow me.'

She grew even more confused. 'You have no mistress?'

'Not at this time.'

'Nor any other…'

'No.'

'Since we married, you have not—'

'I said, no,' he snapped.

'I do not understand.'

'Nor do I,' he responded. 'But that doesn't mean I

wish for you to take a lover after less than a month of marriage. You cannot expect me to sit idly by and do nothing about it.'

Her argument ran out of fuel, and her anger cooled. But his argument became no clearer. And so she said, 'Your friends do not seem overly bothered by their wives' conduct.'

'My friends all have several children. Any inheritances or titles have been assured. Their wives have performed the duties, which you have expressed no interest in. They have earned latitude.'

'And is that the only problem? You think that I encourage Timothy too soon?'

'People will say that turnabout is fair play, and I am getting a taste of what I deserve. And they will question the legitimacy of my heir, should there be one, even if I do not.'

She smiled at the nonsense of it. 'But I have no intention of getting myself with child.'

He shook his head. 'You are wise in many things, but there is much you do not know. Let me try to explain. First, you understand that you do not get yourself with child, it is a collaborative effort.'

'I do not plan to collaborate.'

He sighed. 'If you have feelings for Timothy, or any one else, for that matter, these feelings could lead you to a place where collaboration is inevitable.'

'I am not so easily led, Adam,' she said.

He shook his head. 'At one time, I thought I was as wise as you think you are now. A private conversation, a shared joke, the touch of a hand in friendship, or a waltz or two in public would lead to nothing. It was all innocent flirtation that I could stop before it got out of control. But considering our histories, you should sympathise with how easy it can be to respond poorly in the heat of the moment. And there is much heat in a forbidden kiss.'

He sank down on the couch, his head in his hands. 'The next morning, I realised what I had done, and could not bring myself to look in the mirror. I was too ashamed. And that wasn't the last time. I could not seem to stop it until I had driven myself near to ruin and hurt family and friends with the indiscretion.

'And I am not as noble as my good friend Timothy, to be all understanding and forgiveness. Should he try to do to me what I did to him, I am more like to put a ball through him in the heat of anger than look quietly aside. I do not wish it to end thus.' He looked up at her, in desperation. 'If you truly prefer him to me, tell me now, and I will request the annulment that you once offered. Then you will be free to do as you like.'

'I would make you pay back the money you have used,' she countered.

'You would have no right to do so. An annulment will make it as if you have never been married. Control of your estate would revert to your brother. I think he would consider the debts I incurred to be money well spent. The man would be more likely to kiss me than you would.' He put his hand on hers. 'I do not like Hector, and have no desire to aid him in controlling you, but neither will I allow you to shame me in public or destroy an already fragile friendship.'

She shook her head in amazement. She could not

decide which was stranger: her husband's jealous raving, or the twisted logic of the upper class. 'So if any man speaks to me, you will be convinced that I am unfaithful, like all the other wives. And then you will corner me to rant, as you have tonight, although you have no reason.'

He gave her a sad smile, and nodded.

She continued. 'And although in time you are likely to stray from me, I will be allowed no indiscretions at all, for you do not wish people to think that your heirs are illegitimate. You understand that there is no point in suspecting the legitimacy of your children until you have some?'

And now, he was looking at her with speculation. The silence drew out long between them.

'But if you did, that would mean…' Her pulse quickened in response. 'Oh, no.'

'We could remain unfortunately childless, I suppose. And celibate. And hope that my brother marries and produces. But that is a lot to assume. If there is any hint of infidelity on your part, annulment will continue to be an option.'

'You mean to hold that over my head for the rest of our lives?'

'If necessary.' The intensity of his gaze grew. 'Or we could try another way.'

Her pulse was racing now, as it began to occur to her that he was serious in what he was suggesting. 'That was most definitely not part of the original bargain.'

'When you planned to marry, you must have considered the possibility.'

Strangely, she had not. She had assumed it would be hard enough to get a man to the altar, and that any so doing would not be the least interested in sexual congress with her, if other opportunities presented themselves. But the need for succession had not been part of her plans. And now, Adam was looking at her in quite a different way than he did after political discussions in the study. He was looking at her as a woman, and she remembered what Tim had said to her.

She sat down beside him, afraid to meet his gaze lest he see how she felt about him. 'I'd never have married a duke had I known it would become so complicated.'

'I am sorry to have inconvenienced you,' he said, not the least bit contrite. 'But I will need an heir. Once one has married, it makes sense to look at the obvious solution to the problem.'

'And you would…with me…and we…'

He nodded. 'Two male children are preferable, but one might be sufficient. If it was a boy, and healthy. If the first is a daughter, then…'

'But that would mean…we would…more than once…'

'Most certainly. Repeatedly. For several years at least.'

Repeatedly. She sat there, eyes round, mouth open, mind boggled. Unable to speak at all.

He continued. 'When you think of it, a sacrifice of a year or two, against the rest of your life, is not so long a time. You are rich enough to have nannies and governesses to care for any offspring. It would in no way interfere with your studies, for it must not be too hard

to keep up on reading while in your months of confine-
ment. What else would you have to do?'

'And once you have an heir…'

'Or two,' he prompted.

'Then I am free to do as I like?'

'We both will be. The marital obligations are fulfilled. Gossip is silenced. We can go our separate ways,
as planned, even while remaining under the same roof.'

'Like everyone else.'

'If we wish.'

He was right, which made it all the more maddening. After the initial display of temper, he had presented
his case most rationally. He was not asking more than
an average husband would expect. She had been the one
to make the unreasonable request. But he was quite
upfront about his willingness to return to her plan, once
the niceties were performed. Other than the absolute
terror she felt, when she thought of what they would do
together, she could find no flaw in his logic.

She stared at him. 'And you are willing to…with me.'

'Of course.' He said it as though the fact somehow
answered her question.

'But when we married…there was no plan to… I
never expected that you would want…'

He smiled. 'If I had found the idea repellent, I would
never have agreed to continue with the marriage. And
I will admit, as we have grown familiar with each other,
I have been giving the matter some thought. I have no
wish to force you, of course. But neither can I stand idly
by while you take a lover.'

If he was to be believed, he had been faithful to her,

despite opportunity and temptation, for the brief duration of their marriage. And it must be true, for he would gain nothing by lying, since she did not care.

But if she did not care, then why was the idea so flattering? As was the idea that he was seriously considering... She looked at him, sitting beside her, with the candlelight in his eyes, and the beginnings of a beard shadow on his pale cheek. He was the most beautiful man she had ever seen. She could not help an uncontrollable attraction. It was why she had learned to look at him as little as possible, much as one learned not to stare directly into the sun.

'Are you planning to answer today?' he asked. 'Because you have been quiet for a very long time, and I find it unnerving. If you wish more time to consider, I will understand.'

'No. No, really I am fine.' Tim had said she should let him charm her. And he was only asking her to do what she had secretly wanted for quite some time.

'And?' He made a gesture, as if to coax more words out of her.

'Oh. Yes. And... Well... Although I did not expect it, I do not see anything unreasonable about your request. You are right. I will inform Tim, if he should flirt with me again, that his attentions are inappropriate. And I will...'

He raised his eyebrows, and gestured again.

'Accede to your request for...' she searched for a word that was not too embarrassing '...collaboration.'

He smiled. 'Thank you. Shall we begin?'

'Now?' She slid down the couch to be as far away from him as possible.

'I fail to see why not.' He slid after her to be near to her again, and covered her hands with his. 'I do not mean to take you here, if that is what frightens you. Now that I have your consent, it is not as if we need to rush.'

'Oh.' Her heart was hammering as his hands stoked up her arms, to touch her shoulders.

'But I do find you quite fetching this evening. Which gave rise to the jealousy of a few moments ago. I feared that other men had noticed what I was seeing in you. For how could they not? Can you forgive me?'

She blinked.

'It was foolish of me. You should not have to bear the brunt of my mercurial temper.'

She blinked again, and took a shaky breath.

'I am afraid I have an overly passionate nature. But as such, it would be most out of character for me if I did not try to steal a kiss or two, to celebrate our last night in London and your successful entrance into society.'

'A kiss.' The words came out of her mouth on a sigh. And she nodded.

'Or two.' He reached behind her, to undo the hooks of her gown.

'Then why…?' She started forward, which only brought her closer to his body, and his hands worked to loosen her stays, proving again his knowledge of lady's underthings.

'I have been told that, although they are lovely, ballgowns tend to be rather constricting. It will be easier for you to relax if we undo your lacing.'

'Oh.' Perhaps he was right, for it was becoming difficult to catch her breath, especially when he held her the way he was doing now.

He felt her trembling, and rubbed his cheek against hers and whispered, 'You have not been kissed before?'

'You did, once. When we first came to London.'

He reached out, and took the glasses off the bridge of her nose, folding them up and setting them aside. 'This will be very different, then.' As his lips moved from her temple down to her mouth, she quite forgot to breathe. And her sudden gasp for air pulled his tongue into her open mouth, which, judging by the way he was using it, seemed to be his object, all along.

He pushed her back into the cushions of the couch, and the kiss became harder, and he sucked, to bring her tongue to him, urging her to stroke and lick in return. This was no ordinary kiss, for there was no sweetness in it, just raw desire. And she opened herself to it, loving the feel of him, wanting her and claiming her for his own.

And suddenly she realised the true reason he had opened her gown, for in her movements under him, her breasts had slipped out of the low bodice, and he was massaging them with his hands, and teasing the tips with his fingers, until she squirmed under him. Then his kiss travelled from her chin, to her neck, to her bare shoulder, before his hands cupped her breasts to bring the nipples, one by one, into his mouth. He settled his head against her, and began to suckle at them, the stubble on his chin rough against them, and the hair of his head, so very soft in contrast. His mouth pulled hard upon them, until she was arching her back, and moaning in pleasure. And then she felt the feeling rush through her body until it left her trembling in his arms.

As he looked up and smiled at her, the clock on the mantel struck three. 'That is enough for tonight, I think.'

She tried to ask him what he meant, in stopping, but the words that came out of her were unintelligible.

'Technically, I think I have fulfilled my promise.' He was still smiling. 'For that was one kiss. Two at most. I don't recall stopping at any point in the last hour. Do you?'

An hour? Had it been so long? She shook her head.

'I could go longer, but it is late, and we are travelling tomorrow, as I promised. But your initial response was most favourable. I think it bodes well for our future together.'

Their future? If tonight had been an indication of things to come, then she hoped the future was not distant. 'When?'

His smile broadened. 'I am not sure. There is an art to these things. I would not want to hurry, but neither am I willing to wait too long. Some time after we have gone home, and can lie in our own bed for as long as we like, taking pleasure in each other.' His hand dipped to her skirt, and he raised the hem. 'You may let me know when you are ready.' His fingers trailed up her leg, until they were above her knee and had searched out the top of her stocking. He ran his fingertips lightly along the bare skin above the silk, before untying her garter. The stocking slipped, and he pressed the pad of his thumb against the naked flesh of her inner thigh.

She felt her legs trembling at the touch, and moaned in response.

'Not that way, although it is music to hear, darling.' He pulled the ribbon down her leg and waved it in front of her. 'You will be ready when you are brave enough to take this back from me.' And he tucked it into his coat pocket, and offered her his hand. 'Now sit up, so that I may put your clothing back together, and we will go upstairs to let the maid take it apart again.'

Chapter Sixteen

The next day he sat across from her in the carriage, watching as she watched the road. She was not the uneasy traveller that had returned with him from Gretna. As the city passed away to be replaced by villages and open road, he watched her taking in the changing landscape, returning to her book time and again, only to gaze back out the window. She was as happy in leaving London as a normal woman would be to go there.

He shook his head and smiled to himself. Last night's conversation had been more than strange. If it had been any other woman in the world, the solution would have been easy. The merest suggestion on his part, and an assignation would have been guaranteed. That he should have to explain the obvious, quietly and politely to his own wife, and then wait for her assent, was an idea beyond comprehension.

But he had not realised, until last night, that their plan

to remain apart was a disaster in the making. It had never occurred to him that his wife might have favourites, just as his friends' wives did. That he had no right to expect her fidelity nor method to encourage it had struck him like a thunderclap.

And to see his best friend at her side, so far from the ballroom, had churned up all the feelings of guilt that he had been trying to hide. If only Tim had told him not to be an idiot when he'd questioned him. But he had laughed it off, and given him a knowing look that said, 'It would serve you right.'

Adam must nip it in the bud immediately. He was not without charm. He had been told he was surpassingly handsome. And he was a duke, damn it all, which should be more than sufficient for even the most selective of wives. He would bring the sum total of his experience to bear on the problem and the inexperienced printer's daughter would melt in his hands like butter.

Was already melting, come to that. He'd felt her kisses the previous night, and seen the stricken look she had given him when he'd stopped.

This morning, she sat there, her lips swollen and chapped from his kiss, and watched him when she did not think he would notice. This was much more of what he expected. She had not noticed him before, and he had not realised how it had annoyed him.

Now she was aware. Sexually aware of him. Watching his hands and thinking that they had touched her. Watching his mouth and knowing that it would kiss her again. And wondering about the garter that lay coiled in his pocket, and what she might be willing to do to get it.

He had wondered about that himself. He had imagined her response would be stiff and awkward, and perhaps a little cold. But the image of warm butter was more apt. Hot and delicious.

He licked his lips, and she followed the movement of his tongue with fascination, before looking away and feigning interest in her book.

It would not be too very long before she was as eager to give herself to him as he was to take her. He would do as he willed with her for as long as he liked— for a lifetime, if necessary—and there would be no more of this nonsense about taking lovers and leading separate lives.

And it all would be settled before the first snows fell, and his wife realised that her main sources of entertainment for the long winter months would be visits from his brother Will, and their good neighbour, Tim. He would have no peace in his own home if he could not trust the woman he had married when she was out of his sight. And while he wished, in many things, he could emulate the fine character of his friend, he had no wish to marry for wealth, only to have the woman put horns on him and make him the laughing stock of London.

They pulled into an inn yard for the evening, and he helped his wife from the carriage and told Jem to arrange food for them, a private sitting room, and a single bedroom.

The servant could not hide his brief look of surprise, and followed it with an insolent glare before doing as he was bid. Later, after Penny was safely inside, he caught up with his wife's servant, slouching the baggage toward the rooms. 'Here, fellow. I wish a word with you.'

Jem turned and set the bags on the floor and then straightened. For the first time, Adam noticed the bulk of the man, who stood several inches taller than he did, and was broad and strong of back, despite his advancing age. The servant glared down at him, too close for a bow in the enclosed space of the hallway, and touched his forelock. 'Your Grace?'

'Just now, in the courtyard. I did not like the look you gave me when I gave you instruction.'

'So sorry, your Grace. I will endeavour to improve myself in the future.' But the man was still looking at him as though concluding that one good slap would be all it might take to send the title to Will.

Adam straightened as well, putting on the air of command that served him so well in the House of Lords. 'It is no business of yours where your mistress sleeps. Or if we might choose to put aside the ridiculous arrangement created by Penny in favour of something closer to sanity. From this point forward, we will be acting as other couples do, and not as two strangers pretending to be married.'

Jem's eyes narrowed, and he said, 'Very good, your Grace. Because all intelligent people aspire to a union that is the current mode of the day: full of luxury, casual carnality and pretence, but devoid of any sincere feeling between the parties involved. Unless one is to count the contempt you seem to have for one another. My mistress has never wanted more than her parents had: a true meeting of the minds and a deep and abiding affection, strong enough to transcend the bonds of life itself. When her father died, your Grace, it held no fear for him, for he was convinced that his wife waited for him on the other side. That is what my mistress expected. When she found she could not have it, then she wanted to be left alone, and in peace.'

The servant looked down upon him again, as if he were still face down in the muck of the inn yard. 'And in the end, she will have to settle for you.' He picked up the bags that he had dropped, balanced them easily on his shoulders, and started down the hall. 'This way to your room, your Grace.'

She was waiting for him, there, in the tiny sitting room that connected to the room where they would sleep. A supper had been laid for them on the low table: cold meat pies, cakes, ale for him and tea for the lady.

And as he came to her, she hastily set down the mug of ale, and wiped some foam from her lips. She looked down, embarrassed. 'I'm sorry. You must think me frightfully common.'

He smiled. 'For doing something that you enjoy?'

When she looked back at him, there was fear in her eyes. A desperation to please him that hadn't been there before the party. She hadn't given a damn for what he thought of her then. But things had changed. 'I suspect the wives of your friends do not steal ale from their husband's mug when he is not looking.'

He sat down next to her. 'They do things far worse.' He tasted the ale. 'And this is quite good. We can share it, if you like.' He set the mug between them, and reached for his plate. His sleeve brushed against her arm; instead of shying from him, as she once might have done, she leaned to be closer.

And when she did it, his heart gave a funny little leap in his chest. He covered the feeling by taking another sip of ale. Not knowing how to proceed, he said, 'I spoke to my brother last night as the guests were leaving. Apparently, you told him how your work was progressing.'

She gave a little shake of her head. 'I am afraid I am not very good at small talk. I'm too little in public to have the knack of it.'

'No,' he corrected quickly. 'It was all right. More than all right. He was most impressed by you, and told me so. Still a little surprised, of course, that I found a woman with a brain who would have me.'

She laughed. 'What an idea, that the Duke of Bellston could not attract a woman of intelligence. I used to read the papers, and imagine what it would be like to meet you. I was sure that your wife would need her wits about her at all times if she were to speak to you at all.'

'Then you must have been sorely disappointed to find so little challenge...' He stopped. 'You used to imagine *me*?'

She put her hand to her temple, to hide her embarrassment. 'There. The truth is out. I sat at home reading Greek, and shunning society, spinning girlish fancies over a man who I would never meet. I assumed, by the wisdom of his speeches, he must be long married, and perhaps already a grandfather. I would never dare speak to him. But perhaps, if I could ever find the nerve, I would write to him with a question concerning his position on something or other, perhaps pretending to be my brother, or some other male, and he might deign to answer me.'

'And then you found me drunk in the street, and I hauled you to London and ignored you, and then forced you to dress in ribbons and dance with my friends, while I sat in another room, playing cards.' He laughed until tears came to his eyes, and when he noticed she was still pink with mortification, he pulled her close, and hugged her to him until he felt her laugh as well.

Then he buried his face against her neck, and murmured, 'I hope we are close enough now that, if you have any questions, you will not feel the need to submit them in writing.'

She said, 'I…think whatever I meant to ask you has gone quite out of my head.'

'Speak of something you know, then. For I do love the sound of your voice.' He breathed deeply, taking in the scent of her hair.

'Do you want me to ask for my garter, now?' It was the barest whisper, fearful, but full of hope as well.

And it tugged at his heart, to know how hard she had been trying to be what he wished, and how little he had done to make it easy for her. 'No games tonight.' He put his arms around her. 'Come. Sit in my lap. Tell me about your work. What is it about this Odysseus fellow that makes him worth the attentions of my Penelope?'

She hesitated at first, and then did as he said, wrapping her arms around his neck and whispering the story to him. He relaxed into the cushions of the divan, and thought what a great fool Odysseus must have been to get himself so cursed that he couldn't find his way back, and to waste time with Calypso or Circe when everything he needed was waiting at home.

When she finished, it was late. The fire was low and the candles were guttering. She lay still against him for a moment, and then said, 'I have talked too long.'

He stroked her head, and pulled a pin from her hair. 'Never. But it is time for bed. Let me help you.' He pulled more pins from her hair, uncoiling braids and combing them out with his fingers. He had never seen it down before, and the softness surprised him. He ran his fingers through the length of it, and closed his own eyes. 'Silk. I have never felt anything so soft.'

'It is too fine,' she argued. 'If I do not keep it tied, it tangles.'

He brought the strands to his face, breathing the scent of it and letting it cascade through his fingers. 'I will braid it for you again. Later.'

She reached out to him, and caught the end of his cravat, and undid the knot, letting it slide through her fingers to the floor. The gesture was carelessly erotic, although she seemed to have no idea of the fact. Then she slid from his lap and stood up, starting toward the bedroom and looking back over her shoulder at him.

He rose as well, stripping off his coat and waistcoat, and undoing his shirt. Then he went to stand behind her, and she held her long hair out of the way as he undid her clothing. She was very still as he worked, loosening hooks and lacings, pushing her gown off her shoulders and to the floor, kissing the back of her neck. Then he went to sit on the end of the bed, pulling off his boots and stockings, and undoing the buttons on his trousers.

He looked up at her, still standing where he had left her, the firelight outlining her body through the lawn of her chemise. She was watching him. Her eyes travelled slowly over his body. He could feel her gaze, like the touch of fingers, on his shoulders, his chest, his stomach and lower. Then she removed her glasses, holding them tightly in her hand, and closed her eyes.

He stood up and took them from her. 'Would you like me to put out the lights?'

'Please.'

He set them on the table beside the bed and blew out the candles, one by one, until the room was lit only by the fire. 'There. Now we are both a bit blind, and there is nothing to be afraid of. Remove your shift, and climb into bed.' He removed his trousers, hung them over a nearby chair, then threw back the covers and climbed in himself.

She waited until he was settled, and then quickly stripped off the last of her clothing, draping it over the end of the bed and going around to her side. Her movements were slow and sure, for she had believed him when he said he was near blind. But he could see her well enough: the hair, pale as moonlight, trying and failing to hide her full breasts, slim waist and soft, round hips.

She climbed into the bed, and he threw the covers back over her and pulled her close to bring her forehead to his lips. She trembled a little and so he said, 'Do not worry. I will do nothing tonight that will alarm you. We can wait until we are home to be more intimate. But I wish very much to touch you.'

'And kiss me again?'

'Once or twice.'

'I would like that. Very much.' And she turned her open mouth to his.

He kept his movements slow and gentle. His tongue stroked hers and traced the edge of her teeth, and his hands massaged her neck and her shoulders, making her muscles relax and her body melt into his. He let his hands slide lower down her back, and cupped her to him as he thrust his tongue into her mouth.

Instinctively, she parted her thighs and tried to get closer still, until he had to stop for a moment, to remind himself that he meant to go slowly, and not take what she was offering.

He pushed away from her, rolling her on to her back, and she moaned, reaching to bring him close to her again. He pulled himself up to kneel between her parted legs, and let the covers fall away so that he could watch her as he played with her breasts. If she had been shy of him before, she had forgotten it, and looked up at him with love-drugged eyes as he stroked her, catching her lip between her teeth as he teased her nipples, and stroking her own hands up the sides of her body to squeeze his hands on her, encouraging him to be less gentle.

He took her permission and kneaded and pinched, until she was writhing on the bed, her hips bucking as her body begged to be loved. The sight was making him dizzy with lust and painfully hard.

He fell upon her then, pushing her body back on to the bed, and burying his face against her breasts, letting his teeth do what his fingers had, and sliding his hands between her legs to stroke her, gripping her thighs and spreading them wider, sliding his thumbs up to part the hair and find her most sensitive places. He could feel her heart, beating under his cheek, and waited until he was sure that it must be near bursting it was so loud. And he lifted his face from her breast and swore to her that it would be ever like this between them, if she would trust him and let him love her as she deserved. Then he thrust, filling her with his fingers.

She was hot and tight, and he imagined the feeling of sliding into her body, night after night, and waking to her sweet smile, day after day, knowing that she would always belong to him. And he heard her cry out and collapse against his hand, sated.

He released her and slipped up her body to kiss her upon the mouth again, and she gasped and laughed. 'That was magnificent.'

He rolled off her, and said, 'That was just the beginning. Here, turn over and let me do up your hair.'

'My hair?'

'To give me something else to do with you.' He reached out and pulled the length into a messy braid. Then he wrapped it around her to tease her breasts with the end. 'For if I do the things I am thinking of, we will get no sleep at all, and you will have a most uncomfortable ride tomorrow.'

She yawned. 'That sounds very wicked.' And then she settled back into him, grinding her hips against him, and driving him one step closer to insanity. 'But I am very tired. Perhaps you may show me tomorrow.' She yawned again. 'I think I shall very much want to reclaim my garter.'

'I sincerely hope so.' And he lay back against the pillows and cradled his wife's body to him for a night of delicious agony.

Chapter Seventeen

The next day, Penny watched her husband dozing on the other side of the carriage. He said he had not slept well, but he did not seem overly bothered by the fact.

She, on the other hand, had had an excellent night's sleep. Her body could remember every kiss and every touch from the previous evening, and it woke hungry for more. The feeling was aggravated by the gentle rocking of the carriage. She was excited enough by the prospect of the new home that her husband had described to her. But the nearness of him, and the promise that they would be alone together from now on, left her nearly overcome.

Adam started awake, and looked out of the window, smiling and pointing to a marker that he said indicated the edge of his property.

He leaned his head out of the window of the carriage, closed his eyes, and inhaled deeply. Then he looked sheepishly back at her. 'You will find it embarrassingly sentimental of me, I'm sure. But I find that the air smells sweeter in Wales than anywhere in England. And is not the quality of the sunshine brighter than that in the city?'

She thought to comment on the coal burning in London, and the noise of the traffic, which were impediments to the climate and perfectly rational explanations for the changes he described. If the Welsh air smelled of anything, she suspected it was sheep, for there were flocks in many of the pastures they were passing. She smiled at him. 'Black sheep?'

He grinned at her and nodded. 'Perhaps it is symbolic.' He looked critically at the flocks. 'But there are not as many as there should be. It was a hard winter, with a late spring and a dry summer.' He shook his head.

She looked out the window at the land they were passing. The year had obviously been difficult. The fields and gardens were not as green as she expected them to be, nor the crops as large. But the tenants appeared happy; as the carriage passed, people in the fields looked up and smiled. They dropped curtsies, removed caps and offered occasional shy waves.

And Adam smiled back and surveyed the land with a critical eye and a touch of possessiveness. He had missed it. And no matter how at ease he had seemed in London, he belonged here.

The carriage slowed as it came up the long curved drive and pulled abreast of the house, and he leaned forward in his seat as though his body strained to be even closer to home. When the footman opened the carriage door, he stepped out, forgetting her. He was immediately surrounded by a pack of dogs, barking, wagging and nudging him with wet noses for his attention. He patted and stroked, calling them by name and reaching absently into a coat pocket for treats that he was not carrying.

She watched him from the door of the carriage as he was drawn like a lodestone to the open front door. And even the butler, whose kind were not known for their exuberant displays of emotion, was smiling to see the return of the master of the house.

Adam took a step forwards, and then froze and turned back to her, embarrassment colouring his face. He strode back to the carriage and reached up to offer her his hand to help her down, making a vague gesture that seemed to encompass his brief abandonment of her. Then he laughed at himself and kicked the step out of the way, held both hands out to her and said, 'Jump.'

She stared at him in amazement. 'Why ever for?'

'Trust me. I will catch you.'

She shook her head. 'This is nonsense.'

'Perhaps. But the sooner you do it, the sooner it will be done. Now, do as I say.'

He showed no sign of relenting, and at last she closed her eyes, and stepped from the carriage into open air.

He caught her easily under the arms, and let her slide down his body until her slippered feet were standing on his boots. The closeness of their bodies was shocking, and she meant to pull away, but he was smiling down at her with such ease that a part of her did not wish to move ever again.

He said softly, 'There are customs about brides and

thresholds, are there not? You must not stumble, or it would be bad luck to us both.'

She pointed to the house. 'I see no reason to hold to superstition. There is nothing wrong with my legs, and the way is not strewn with disaster. I think I can manage.' But it felt good to be held so close to him.

'You have been very lucky for me, up 'til now. It is better to be safe than sorry. Perhaps it were best if I were to see you safely into the house.' And before she could object, he scooped an arm beneath her knees and had lifted her into his arms.

She surprised herself by squealing in delight. She should have demanded that he let her down immediately, and that it was all highly undignified. But instead, she wrapped her arms around his neck, tipped back her head and laughed into the Welsh sunshine. The crowd of dogs still milling about them had to jump to nudge and sniff her as well. And even as he took care to guide her through the pack, she could feel the strain of his body, wanting to go faster and take the last few steps at a run to be inside his house again.

As they passed the butler, the man bowed to her as well as her husband, and murmured, 'Your Grace, welcome home. And welcome to you as well, your Grace. May I offer my congratulations?'

Adam nodded, as though his heart were too full to speak, and held her even closer, before taking the last step that brought them both into the house. Then he set her down and took her by the hand to lead her into the entry, where the servants were assembled.

The introduction was easier than it had been on the

first day in the townhouse, and she hoped that this was a sign that she was adjusting to her new role as well. Although it might have had something to do with the change in the man beside her, who was neither as distant nor as superior. When he smiled with pride as he spoke to the staff, she had a hard time distinguishing whether it was happiness with them, or his eagerness for them to meet her. And she could not help but smile as well.

At last, he held out his hand in a broad gesture and said, 'Your new home,' as though the manor were a person and the introduction would result in a response.

She looked up at the high ceilings, and the wide marble steps that led to the second floor of rooms and a portrait gallery above them.

She could feel his hesitation next to her. He wanted her to like it. And how could she not? It was the grandest house she'd ever seen. Although the idea that it was to be her home was faintly ridiculous.

'The roof needs new slate,' he said in apology. 'But that is the way it is with all old homes. Something is always in need of repair. And nothing has been done in decoration for many years. But the part that is undamaged by the fire is warm and clean, and I find it most comfortable.'

Comfortable? She looked at him. If one found museums to be a comforting place, perhaps. But museums were not so different really than… 'May I see the library?' she asked hopefully.

'Certainly. I believe your books have already arrived.' He led her down the hall and opened a door before them.

She poked her head into the room. Books. Floor to ceiling. Some shelves were so high that a set of brass steps was necessary to reach them. But there was plenty of space for the contents of the crates that stood stacked by the door. A fire had been laid in the grate, and the warmth of it extended to the oak table at the middle of the room. There was space for her papers, ample lamps to light the words. Comfortable chairs by the fireside where she could read for pleasure when she was not working. And the heavy rug beneath her feet was so soft and welcoming that she was tempted to abandon the furniture and curl up upon it.

'Will there be sufficient room for your collection, or shall we need to add extra shelves?'

Without thinking, she had been counting the empty places, and reordering the works. 'There is ample room, I am sure.'

'And here.' He walked to a shelf by the window, and pulled down a battered volume. 'You will not need it, for I think you are well stocked in this. It is left over from my own school days.' He looked at it sadly. 'Which means it has seen very little use.' He handed her a schoolboy's edition of Homer, in the Greek.

She stared down at the book in her hand, and then up to the man who had given it to her. When he was at home, he was a very different person. No less handsome, certainly. The light from the windows made his hair shine, and his eyes were as blue as they had been. But the cynical light in them had disappeared. He seemed younger. Or perhaps it was that he did not seem as arrogant and unapproachable after the previous night.

'It is all right, then? Do you think you can be happy here?'

Happy? It was a paradise. She hardly dared speak.

'Of course, there is more. I haven't shown you your rooms yet.' He led the way out of the library and down the corridor.

She peered in the next room as they passed.

'My study,' he answered. And this time, he opened the door wide so that she could see the desk within. 'It connects to the library. As does the morning room on the other side. I had thought, perhaps you might wish to use it as well, should the library not prove to have sufficient space.' He backtracked down the hall and opened another door. 'It is rather…' He waved a hand at the decoration, which was rococo with gilt and flowers, and a ceiling painted with cherubs and clouds. 'My mother, again.' He looked at her. 'And there are more of the damn china shepherds.'

She reached out to touch a grouping that was very similar to the one she had left in London, a court couple, locked for ever in passionate embrace. She ran a finger along it and felt the heat of the kiss in her body. 'That is all right. I think I am growing used to them.'

He gestured her out of the room and led her down more halls to a music room, separate rooms for dining and breakfast, another parlour, and a formal receiving room. Then he took her up the stairs past the portraits of his family to a long row of bedrooms and opened a door near the end. 'This is to be your room. If you wish.'

It was beautifully appointed, and larger than the one

in the townhouse, but of a similar layout. She looked for the connecting door that should link her room to his. 'And where do you sleep?'

He looked away. 'I am not particularly sure. I had used this room, for a while. But I could choose another. Here, let me show you.' He took her into the hall and opened the door to what must have been the master suite. A strong smell of smoke crept out into the hallway.

He sniffed. 'Better than it was, I'm afraid. The real damage is farther down the hall. But your room is not affected. Let me show you the worst of it.' He seemed to steel himself, gathering courage, then led her down the corridor to the left, and as they walked the odour of smoke got stronger. The line of tension in her husband's back increased. He quickened his pace as they reached the end of the corridor, and threw open the heavy double doors at the end.

He caught her, before she could attempt entrance, for there was little floor to step on. The hall seemed to end in open air before him. She was looking down into what must have been the ballroom before the fire. The light in the room had a strange, greasy quality as it filtered through what was left of the floor-to-ceiling windows on the back of the house. Some of the panes were missing, leaving spots of brightness on the floor and walls. Some were boarded shut, and some merely smoke-stained and dirty. At the second-floor level, there were bits of floor and gallery still clinging to the outer walls. From a place near the roof, an interloping bird sang.

'Oh, my.'

'It was beautiful once,' Adam remarked, bitterness in his voice. 'The retiring rooms were off this hall, card rooms and galleries for musicians. A staircase led up from there.' He pointed to a blank space opposite them.

'How did it happen?'

'There was an accident. After a ball. One of the candleholders was overbalanced, and the flames touched the draperies.' He stopped and swallowed, then started again. 'The truth. You should hear it all, before we go further. It was I who caused it. The party was over, and most of the guests had gone. And I followed Clarissa to the second floor, so that we could be alone. My room is just down the hall and I thought…' He could not look at her, as he spoke. 'But she chose the musicians' gallery. I had too much wine that night, and was thinking too slowly to realise that the acoustics would be excellent. Tim was searching for her, to take her home. He must have heard it all. She made no effort to be quiet that night. And when I cautioned her, she laughed and asked what did I think she'd meant to happen.

'I pushed her away from me, and she overturned the candles. I pulled her clear of the fire, but the flames spread quickly. Fortunately, the walls on this side of the house are old and stone. The damage was limited to this room, and the rooms above and below. And smoke damage to my bedroom, of course. Divine justice.'

'Was anyone hurt?'

Adam seemed to flinch at the thought. 'Will has a burn on the back of his arm, gained from fighting the fire. A beam fell upon him.'

She looked up at the roof, and the badly patched holes, and piles of new lumber on the floor below. 'And this is why you needed the money?'

'Not a thing has gone right since the night of the fire. It was as if I was cursed. I invested. Badly, as it turns out. In tobacco. The ship sank, and my hopes with it. The profits should have been enough to repair the house and account for the failure of this year's crop.' He reached out and took her hand. 'And then I met you. Before that, I had no idea how to go on.'

She looked at him, and at the wreckage before them. 'And you swear, this is over.'

He smiled sadly. 'Nothing brings you to the knowledge that you are behaving like a fool quite so fast as burning your house half to the ground, and seeing your brother nursing injuries that were a result of your stupidity in chasing after another man's wife. And I saw the look on Tim's face that night. Yet he insists on forgiving me, which is the worst punishment of all.'

She tugged at his sleeve. 'Close the doors on this mess, then. Let us go downstairs and find supper.'

Chapter Eighteen

He took her to the formal dining room, which was set for two. And she watched as the servants went through their paces, attempting to impress their new mistress with speed of service and excellence of presentation.

She wondered what Jem thought of it all, and if they had managed to force some work out of him, or had he found a warm corner somewhere to sleep. Perhaps she could find a post for him, something that involved short hours and long naps.

And while her husband might think of them as being totally alone in Wales, she found the room crowded with servants. There were footmen behind each chair and a regular influx of courses arriving and departing. She watched Adam, who was staring at the contents of his plate, but doing very little with it. He must think himself alone, for he seemed to have forgotten her entirely. Instead, he cast furtive glances in the direction of the damaged wing, as though he could sense it through the walls.

By the look in his eyes, he had been wrong. He might think that things were over, and managed to keep them at bay when he was in London and could keep busy enough to ignore them. But his good spirits had begun to evaporate the moment he had opened the door to the ballroom. She wondered how many rooms of the house held bad memories for him. She imagined Clarissa, as Tim had described her, attempting to trap Adam in an indiscretion. The music gallery had been an excellent choice, if she wished discovery.

But had it been the first attempt? Or had she taken every opportunity she could to embarrass her husband and create talk? Penny might be forced to see her own husband starting at ghosts of memory in every room of their home.

Why must the woman have been so beautiful and so audacious? So without shame as to be unforgettable? How was she expected to compete? When they were together, in the inn, Penny had felt like the only woman in the world to him. And in scant hours, he had forgotten her.

The idea angered her, and she prepared to count, when it occurred to her that, in fighting this battle, a measured and thoughtful response would not win the day. If she thought at all, she would never have the nerve to act.

She looked back at Adam, who was staring into his dessert in confusion, as though wondering where the earlier courses had got to. She slid her chair closer to his, so that they might not be overheard. 'Adam. Darling. I was wondering if you had given thought as to where we would sleep?'

He started, and looked up at her. 'I am sorry. I had forgotten. You must be tired after such a long journey. You will take the mistress's suite, of course. I will find somewhere.' He shrugged. 'One of the guest rooms. I doubt I will sleep well this first night.' He gave her a tight, pained smile. 'I had hoped to be in better spirits. There are uneasy memories. But do not let me disturb you.'

She pulled her chair closer still, until their knees were touching under the table. 'You are disturbing me very much, husband. For I was rather under the impression that you would be disturbing me tonight. And I find the prospect of a lack of disturbance…most disturbing.'

He started again, as if waking from a bad dream. 'You still wish…' He raised his eyebrows.

'To reclaim my garter. If you still have it, of course. The way you are acting, I am beginning to suspect that you have forgotten where it is.'

He looked at her, with the long slow smile he used to charm her into so many things, and said, 'I have it on my person, at this moment.'

She took a large sip of wine, to steady her nerves. 'Really? I do not believe you. Show it to me.'

The roguish light was back in his eyes again. 'You must find it for yourself, if you are so curious to see it.'

She toyed with her glass and gauged the locations of the servants, and how much they were likely to see. It was some small consolation that, should any word reach the outside about the indiscretions of the Duke of Bellston, from now on they would involve the duchess as well.

Then she took another drink, casually dropped her hand below the table as though to adjust her napkin, and ran her fingers up her husband's leg.

He choked on his water and gripped the edge of the table. When he had regained his breath, he whispered, 'What the devil are you doing?'

'What you suggested I do,' she whispered back. 'Where else would you wear a garter? You know where it was when you removed it.' Her hand travelled farther up his thigh and his face went white as the blood left it.

'But I do not feel anything.' She gathered all her nerve and thought about last night at the inn. And then she sent her hand higher up his thigh, under his napkin, and undid two of the buttons on his trousers, slipping her hand into the gap. After a few seconds she said, 'And while this is very interesting, I do not think it is a garter, either.'

'Out!'

She sought to remove her hand, but he pressed down on it through the napkin, trapping it where it was.

He turned his head to the footmen at the door, 'Go. All of you. We do not need you. Thank the cook. Wonderful meal. But no more. Do not bother to clear away, just go. And lock the door behind you.'

When he heard the click of the latch, he sighed and leaned back in his chair. Then he closed his eyes and said in a hoarse voice, 'You may continue looking.'

She undid some more buttons, moved the napkin, and peeked beneath the table. When he caught her looking, she said, 'Last night, it was very dark. And I was not wearing my glasses.'

'Oh.'

His response to what she had said sounded quite like a moan, and she smiled in triumph. She looked again, as she felt him shuddering under her hand as she stroked him. 'Shall we play hot and cold?'

'Very hot,' he murmured, and tore at the knot on his cravat.

'I am still looking for the garter, silly. I do not think you have it hidden here at all.'

With one hand, he yanked at the buttons on his waistcoat, and the other cupped the back of her head, dragging her mouth to his for a desperate kiss. When his chest was bare, he pulled her empty hand to his heart, and she stroked the hair on his chest, and the nipples hidden in it. He broke the kiss and guided her mouth down to them, letting her bite and suck as he had done for her, while he fumbled at the closures on her gown, swearing as he fought to dispense with her clothes.

Had she unbalanced him to that degree? A feeling of power rushed through her, along with desire, and she could feel her body readying itself for what was to come. Her breasts ached to be touched, and as she stroked him she could feel the heat building inside her, where he would soon be.

She stopped what she was doing and enjoyed the moment, and then looked at her husband. She'd thought him a master of seduction. But tonight the tables were turned, and he could not undo the simple knot that held her stays in place. 'Really, Adam. If you cannot manage, perhaps I shall go to my room and send for the maid.'

'You will do no such thing.' He grabbed her hands and placed them firmly on his knees, bending her over the arm of his chair. 'Do not move.' And then he seized a knife from the table in front of them, and slit the lacings of her corset from bottom to top.

She sat up and took a deep breath, which he stole with another kiss and then pulled the thing free of her, and threw it on to the floor. She stood up and let the gown follow it, and then he grabbed her by the waist and lifted her to sit on the table, kissing her face, her throat and her breasts. Between the kisses he undid the last button on his trousers. Pushing them out of the way, he panted, 'Sorry, darling. Most undignified. And not as gentle as I should be. I cannot help myself.'

He could not help himself. And he was talking to her. She took a breath to calm her nerves, and then pulled up her chemise and spread her legs, leaning back to tip her hips up. 'Stop talking and take me.'

'Say that you love me,' he whispered. 'I want to hear you say the words.'

And it was surprisingly easy to tell him the truth. 'I love you,' she whispered back.

This time, he was the one to groan, 'Soon.' And he kissed her again, rough and insistent. So she reached out and put her hand to him again, and mimicked the strength of his kiss. She could feel herself losing the boundary between what she was feeling, and what he must be feeling as he found her with his fingers and thrust.

She rocked her hips against his hand, and let him fill her, as the feelings grew inside of her, and his sex grew slippery in her palm.

'Very soon,' he whispered. His hips thrust toward hers until the head of his sex rested against her, and she writhed against it, stroking so that it rubbed her body where it felt most right. She was trembling with excitement, balancing on the edge of something wonderful. He removed his fingers from her, clutching her hip with his hand to steady her, and bring her closer to him.

The emptiness frustrated her, and she stroked harder, feeling him tremble, and rubbed herself with him until his sex slipped against the opening to her body, making her gasp.

And he said, 'Now,' and drove into her.

There was a shock of pain, and he kissed her until it hardly mattered, and the tension grew in her again. He pushed her back to brace her hands on the table so that her hips stayed steady, put his hands on her breasts and thrust, over and over again, staring into her eyes.

She leaned back and wrapped her legs around him so that the friction of their bodies changed, driving her wild with touches that were never long enough. But they brought her close again, so very close. And when he shuddered against her and stopped, she moaned in protest until he stroked her with his thumb and took her over the edge.

When she came back to herself, they had moved very little. She held him inside her, her legs wrapped around his waist, and he was leaning over her on the table, staring down into her face.

He dropped a kiss on her lips, and glanced around the shambles they had made of dinner. What clothing they had managed to remove was scattered around them, chairs were tipped, and goblets were knocked over on the table. He reached beside her, and fed her a candied apricot from the dessert tray, watching her mouth with interest as she ate. 'In case you are wondering,' he said, 'I had intended something a bit more sedate for our first evening together.'

'Oh, really?' she touched her tongue to her lips, and waited as he offered her a bit of cake.

He furrowed his brow. 'I believe my original plan was to seduce you at my leisure, and render you docile and agreeable through lust.'

'And my garter?'

'Is tied around my shirt sleeve, for I thought, perhaps, you would summon the nerve to help me off with my jacket.'

'And what do you think of your plan now?' She shifted her legs to grip him tighter.

He sighed and smiled. 'It is an utter failure. You control me body and soul. Command me.' And he looked supremely happy to have lost.

She released him, and offered her hand to him, so that he could help her down from the table. 'Take me to our bedroom.'

His smile broadened and he scooped up her dress and tossed it over her head. Laughing and whispering, they collected the rest of the discarded clothing and a plate of cakes. Then he opened the door, checked the hall to make sure it was empty and they ran from the room together, not stopping until they were safely behind the closed bedroom door.

Chapter Nineteen

Adam came down to the breakfast room and took his usual seat. His coffee was already poured, the mail was stacked beside the plate, and his wife was seated at his side. Life was as close to perfect as any man had a right to expect.

Penny was as happy in Wales as he had known she would be, even more so now that they had each other. For a month, they had awoken every morning, tangled in the sheets and each other, breakfasted together, and then he went to his study, and she to the library. He could read his paper, ride out to inspect the property, or argue with the workmen who had begun renovations on the ballroom, knowing that when he came back, his steadfast Penelope would be waiting for him.

They had not yet made love in the library, perhaps because he had spent so little time there, before Penny had come to the house. She had learned the measure of him, on that first night. And now, if she felt he was growing morose, or attempting to dwell in the past, she had but to lock the door and show him a flash of garter, and he was lost to the world.

But any suggestions made in the library would be of his own doing. He looked up into her face, startled by the thought, and smiled as he caught her looking at him.

'Excuse me?'

'What?'

'Was there something…?'

They spoke in unison, to cover their mutual confusion, and fell silent at the same time.

'The eggs,' he lied. 'I bit down on a piece of shell.'

'I will speak to Cook.'

'Do not worry, it is nothing.'

She nodded and looked down into her plate.

'They are very good eggs today,' he supplied. 'The best I have ever tasted, I think.'

'You say that every morning.' She went back to her breakfast. But she was blushing.

At some point, he would have to return to London, or share her with the world. But not just yet. For now, they were the only two people on earth, and it was enough. He opened the first letter on the stack, and a folded sheet dropped on to his plate.

…torment me no longer. For I cannot live without the perfection of your body, the taste of your kiss, the sound of your voice as you call my name…

He recognised his own hand, and remembered the letter well. It had been drunken folly to have written it.

He should have thrown it on the fire rather than sent it. And it was hardly the most damning thing he put to paper in the months before the fire.

It was accompanied by another sheet, with a single line.

Come to me at Colton, or I shall go to her.
Clare

She had followed them to Wales.

'Something interesting in the mail?' Penny did not look up from her tea.

'Nothing important.' Perhaps he had grown better at concealing his feelings from her, for she did not seem to notice that the room had gone cold, or that his mouth had filled with smoke and ashes.

'Then I will leave you to it, and return to work.' She raised her eyebrows. 'Ithaca calls.'

'With its rosy fingers of dawn?'

'There must be a better way to say that,' she said, and wandered down the hall, lost in thought.

He stared back at the letter in front of him, and then threw it into the fireplace, watching the edges curl and the words disappear. He poked at the bits of ash until there could be nothing left of them to read.

Then he went to the stables to saddle a horse.

The Colton property abutted his, and as he rode toward it, he could feel the tightening in his chest. He should have spoken the truth to Penny, and got it over with. Soon she would be seeing Clarissa again, and that it would be impossible to avoid contact, if the Coltons had returned to Wales.

But it was very unlike them to be here in the summer. Clare much preferred Bath. He had not been prepared for the letter, and he had no response at hand. Perhaps the situation was not as bad as it seemed. He could assess, and return to Penny by lunch, with an explanation.

Tim's house seemed as it always did, preternaturally quiet. There was nothing to indicate that the family was in residence, although what he expected to find, he was not sure. Tim must be out riding in the hills. Probably trying to avoid his wife.

The servant allowed him entrance and took him to the sitting room without introduction.

Clare was waiting for him, lounging on a divan in dishabille, her dressing gown artfully arranged to display a length of bare leg, the globe of a breast, and the barest hint of nipple, peeking from the ruffles of lace. 'Adam. At last.'

Her voice raised the hairs on the back of his neck, just as it always did, and he wondered how he could have mistaken the feeling for passion. 'Clarissa. Why have you come here?'

'Because it is my home.'

'It is Tim's home. And you loathe it. You have told us often enough.'

'Then I will be honest. I came because I missed you.' She pulled a pretty pout, which made her look more like a spoiled child than a seductress. 'It has been so long.'

'Barely a month.'

'Why did you leave London?'

'You should know that. I sought to be where my wife would be happiest.' *And to be where you were not.*

'Timothy would not let us travel home to be near you. He insists on staying in the city, although it is unbearably hot, and everyone of fashion is leaving.'

'Go to Bath, then. Somewhere that suits you.'

She sighed. 'I did not want Bath. I longed for the comforts of home. If he does not wish to follow, I cannot very well force him. He may stay in the city with the children for all I care.'

'You left your husband and your children as well.' Adam shook his head in disgust.

She shifted, allowing her robe to fall open, so that there could be no mistake of her plans for the next hour. 'I am totally alone, if you still fear discovery. My servants know better than to talk. And your wife spends most days poring over her books, does she not? No one will be the wiser.'

'I thought I made it clear that there would be nothing more between us.'

'On the contrary. You think that by saying nothing, and running away from me, you can end what we had together. If you truly wanted to end it, you would have told me so, outright. But I think you are afraid to speak to me. You are still not sure what you will say to me, Adam, when we are alone. And I have your letters, you know. I read them often. I know the contents of your heart.'

He felt a wave of humiliation, remembering the things he had written to her. Words he wished he'd have saved for the woman who deserved them. 'That is all in the past, Clare. If you must hear me speak the truth plainly, before you believe it, then listen now. Anything that there was between us is at an end. I will not come crawling back to you like a whipped dog. I have a wife now.'

'Why should it matter? I have always had a husband, and it did not seem to bother you.'

The mention of Tim cut at his heart. 'It bothered me a great deal, Clarissa. He is my friend.'

'And I am your lover.'

'Do not dignify what we did by calling it love. There was no higher feeling involved than lust. I disgusted myself with my behaviour.'

She laughed. 'You did not seem so disgusted at the time, as I remember it.'

'I betrayed Tim. That was why you were so eager to snare me, was it not? You enjoyed our liaisons all the more, for knowing how it would hurt your husband.'

'I viewed it as a challenge,' she admitted. 'To see if my charms were strong enough to break your fragile sense of honour. And it snapped like a twig. Now you think silence, distance and a hasty marriage is all it will take to gain your freedom.

'Do you not remember trying this trick before with me? The cold silence. You lasted for six months. And when you came back, I made you beg before I would let you share my bed.' She tipped her head to the side and smiled in remembrance. 'It was really quite amusing. I wonder what I shall make you do this time, once you grow bored with your shop clerk and you want me again.'

He heard the words and, for the first time in months, everything came clear. Suddenly, as if a bond had been cut, he felt truly free of her. And it was his turn to laugh. 'You trapped me well, with your sly affections and your subtle advances. You came to me when I was most vulnerable, when I was troubled, or lonely, or too drunk to care what I was doing. You used my weaknesses against me and took what you wanted. And afterwards, you left me broken. Cursed by my actions, ashamed of what I had become.

'But when Penny found me in that state, she gave herself to me until I was healed. She has made me, in a few short weeks, into the man I wished I was. I can never give her what she truly deserves, for nothing I have is equal to her casual generosity towards me.

'I love her, Clarissa. And I never loved you.'

She laughed back at him. Long and hard and unladylike. 'Never mind, then. For she appears to have made you into the very thing I abhor. The virtuous prig that you never were, before you met her. Your head is full of romantic nonsense. What you mistake for sincerity is emotional claptrap. I wash my hands of you.'

He felt a flood of relief. And then he saw her smile, which was sly and catlike, and knew that there was no chance in the world that he would escape so easily.

She continued. 'Since your love for her is true, I assume that you have her heart as well. So she will stand by you, head held high, while I reveal the particulars of our relationship to the world. You detailed in writing what we had done, and what you wished to do. I could send the letters to your wife, as a belated wedding gift. Or shall I leave them for Timothy some morning, mixed up with the mail? Or I could take them to our friends in London, to read aloud. Everyone will find it most diverting, I am sure.'

The idea of it turned his stomach. There was so much shame to be had in his past behaviour. Heaps of disgrace for all concerned. Timothy would no longer be able to feign ignorance, and must be moved to act. He would meet his best friend at dawn with a weapon in his hand, and attempt to defend himself for an indefensible action.

Will would shake his head in pity, as he had at the news of the marriage, and at all the other stupid things Adam had done in his life. Perhaps Adam was destined to be an eternal source of disappointment, and a terrible example to his brother.

But Penny. If Penny found out, it would be worst of all. Would she be more hurt by a full revelation from Clare, or would the *ton* throw the information back in her face some night, when she least expected it? Either way, it did not seem likely that she would wish to make love to him in the library, once she knew all the sordid details of his affair. She might return to her study and never venture forth again.

And the worst of it was that the truth could leave him relatively untouched. What did it matter what people said of him? For no matter how shocked the world might be, he was Bellston until he died.

But it would wound the people most dear to his heart.

What were the alternatives? He could return to Clarissa, to buy her silence for a time, and hope that she would grow bored enough to let him go. It would hurt the same people just as much, if not more. For how could he claim that his infidelity was meant to lessen the damage? There was no easy answer. But the choice between right and wrong was clear. Better to bear the agony, lance the wound, and allow the poison to drain, than to leave things as they were, dying from within.

He opened his eyes and stared at Clarissa. 'Do your worst, then. I should have expected no less from you, for you are wicked to the bone. Bring down the ruin upon my head. It is just as I have deserved, and I have known for a long time that there was no preventing it. What will happen will happen. But do not think that you can control me any longer with the fear of revelation. Whatever may occur, I am through with you, Clarissa.'

And he turned and left the room, feeling lighter than he had, despite the sense of impending doom.

Chapter Twenty

Penny sat in the library, watching the blur of sunlight through the leaded windows, as she cleaned her glasses with her handkerchief. Her husband had been right: the air was sweeter here, and the sunshine more bright than any place else on earth.

And then a shadow fell upon her table. Timothy Colton stood, blocking the light from the door.

She smiled and stood, reaching out for his hand. 'Timothy. Whatever are you doing in Wales?'

He was leaning against the door frame, and as her vision cleared, she took note of his appearance. He was the worse for both drink and travel. His hair was wind-blown, his coat dirty, and he smelled of whisky, though it was not yet noon. 'I live here, as does Clarissa. We are near enough to walk the distance on a clear day.' He smiled mirthlessly. 'Did your husband not tell you of the fact?'

She racked her brain, hoping that there had been a revelation, and that she had forgotten. 'No.'

'Now, why do you suppose he would forget to mention it?'

There had to be a reason. He had said that Tim was a childhood friend. And she knew that Clarissa had been there, the night of the fire. But had he told her they would be neighbours? He must have assumed she would know. 'I am sure it was a harmless omission.'

'Really. Then he did not tell you, this morning, that he has gone to my home, to be with my wife.'

'He would not,' she said.

'I was there, and saw them together myself.'

'You lie.'

'When have I ever lied to you, Penelope, that you would distrust me now?' His voice was colder than she'd ever heard it, but he did not avoid her gaze, as her husband had that morning at breakfast. 'She left me in London several days ago. When I realised where she would go, I shut up the house and came after her. It is not so easy when you have children. You cannot simply hare off to Wales, and abandon them to be with your lover. Not that my wife would care.'

'But Adam has not been with her, I would swear it.'

'His horse is in my stables now. And as I approached the house, I could see them clearly through the windows of the sitting room.'

She shook her head. 'I'm sure there is an innocent explanation for it.'

'She was lying bare before him, Penny. There was nothing innocent about the scene I witnessed.'

'Then I will ask Adam about it, when he returns.' She would do nothing of the kind. She would do her best to pretend that it did not matter to her. Perhaps Adam had eyes only for her because she was the only one near enough to see. But she had convinced herself that there would be no worries in the future. It would always be just as it had been for the last month. Now Timothy meant to spoil it all.

'And now I wish you to leave.'

He stepped around her, and shut the door. 'I am not through speaking.'

'I have nothing to say to you. If you wish to talk to anyone, it should be Adam or your wife.'

Timothy laughed. 'And now you will pretend that your husband's affairs do not hurt you. I think this matters more than you care to admit.'

'What business is it of yours?' she snapped.

'If your husband does not wish to be faithful to you? It can be very lonely, knowing that one's chosen mate has little interest. Now that you have had a taste of what marriage might mean, you will find it is very difficult to content yourself with solitude.'

'On the contrary, I much prefer to be alone.'

'If that is true, you are likely to get your wish. But Adam likes company. He is not alone this morning, any more than my wife is. Perhaps it does not matter to you, as a woman, to see your vows tossed back in your face. But I am tired of standing alone while my friend makes me a cuckold again.'

It amazed her, after all they had said to each other, after all they had done, that her husband could be so cruel. 'Challenge him, if you care so much.'

'Do you want us to duel?'

'No.'

Timothy sagged against the wall. 'Strangely, neither do I. Our friendship is over, of course. But I have pretended for so long that I did not care, that it seems foolish now to reach for a sword.' He was staring at her with a strange light in his eyes, as he had the night of the ball.

'Do you mean to reach for me, instead?' she asked.

He sighed. 'There is nothing we can do to stop them, should they wish to be together. But there is no reason for us to be alone.'

'We will be alone,' she responded. 'If we feel anything for them, we will be alone.'

'But we could be together, in shared misery.'

She shook her head. 'I am sorry. I cannot…'

He smiled, and removed a flask from his pocket, taking a deep drink. 'I thought not. And it is truly a shame, Penelope. For I feel I could grow most fond of you, should I allow myself to.' His voice was low and welcoming. 'You are a lovely woman with a quick wit and a sweet nature. You are too good for Adam, my dear. He has many admirable qualities, and has been a true friend in many things. But he is proving to have no more sense than he ever did, when it comes to women. I thought that you brought a change in him.'

'I hoped…' She choked on the words. 'I did not mean to, you know. It was all to be so easy. We both had what we wanted. And then I fell in love with him.'

'There, now.' He reached for her and drew her into an embrace that was more brotherly than passionate. 'Do not cry over him. He is not worth your tears.'

'Oh, really?' Her husband's voice from the doorway was cold.

She sprang back from Timothy's grasp, and hastily wiped at her face with her sleeve.

'It was nothing, Adam,' Penny murmured.

'Other than that you are making this poor woman miserable with your careless philanderings,' Timothy supplied.

'Hush.' Penny cringed at the description of her feelings, hauled out into the light for all to see. 'I was overwrought. It was nothing.'

'Nothing?' Adam stared at her. 'When I find you in the arms of another man, it is not "nothing", madam.'

'She was crying over you,' Tim goaded. 'I could not very well leave her, could I? Although you seemed to have no problem with it.'

'And I suppose, when it comes to comforting my wife, you are worth two of me?' Adam glared at his friend.

'Much as you are, when it comes to my wife.' Timothy glared back. 'Of course, you would have to be as good as two men, for you seem intent on keeping both women. It is hardly fair, old man.' Timothy grinned, but the smile was cold and mirthless.

'I do not want your wife.'

'That was not how it appeared this morning, Adam. After you swore that it was over and you would not be alone with her again.'

Adam made to speak, but hesitated.

Timothy nodded. 'You cannot look me in the eye and deny it, can you?'

'I was with her,' Adam admitted grudgingly. 'But it was nothing. I swear it, Tim.'

The tears rose in her throat as her husband declared his innocence to his friend. But not to her. Never to her, for she did not deserve it. She had sold the rights to his fidelity for a pile of books.

'Do you take me for a fool? I saw you plain, through the window. She was naked before you, in broad daylight.'

'It was not as it appears.'

'It never is,' Timothy responded drily. 'I believe you said that the night of the fire, as well. And I heard the whole thing clearly, although I did not see. Can you not, for once, favour me with the truth? I will at least admit that, given a little more time and the co-operation of your wife, the scene you witnessed, which was truly nothing, would have been exactly what it appeared.'

'How dare you.' Adam's fury was cold. He appeared ready to strike and Penny rushed to his side to take his arm.

'Adam, nothing happened. And no one knows of any of this. Please.'

Tim laughed, 'So what are we to do, then? Do you wish to challenge me, or should I challenge you?' And then he muttered something in Welsh that she did not understand, and spat upon the floor.

She might not have understood the words, but Adam clearly had, for he broke free of her and struck his friend, knocking him to the ground. Tim staggered to his feet with blood in his eye, ready to fight.

And at last, Penny snapped. 'You may do as you please, the both of you. And Clarissa as well. But whatever you do, you can do it without my help.'

'Penny, go to your room.' Adam barely looked at her.

'That is how it is to be, is it? You will be brother and guardian to me, and banish me to my quarters, so that you can do as you please? Take my money, then. I offered it to you freely, in exchange for peace and freedom. And I have scant little of either. But the money was not enough for you. You wanted my affection when it suited you, so that I did not embarrass you in public. And then, you needed my body to be a mother to your children. And now you expect my loyalty, while you lie with another man's wife.

'I want none of it, Adam. No more than I ever did. I want to be alone. And I would sooner see my children raised by jackals than by you or your twisted friends. I am leaving you.'

'You cannot. I will not permit it.' Her husband had turned away from his friend, no longer caring for the fight before him.

'And you cannot stop me. The bargain between us is irretrievably broken. If you thwart me today, I will try again tomorrow. Sooner or later, I will succeed in escaping you. If you wish, you may drag me back to your home by the hair, and lock me in my room. The Duke of Bellston, charming, handsome, lecherous and debauched, will need to keep his wife, and her fortune, by force. And then we will see what people say of you and your precious reputation.'

And she swept from the room.

Chapter Twenty-One

Adam thought, all things considered, that he should feel much worse. But he felt nothing. She had left the room, and taken his anger with her.

He had turned back to Tim, who must have been more than a little drunk, for he had collapsed back on to the floor, and absently offered him a hand.

Tim had ignored it and struggled to his feet, wiping blood from his mouth and on to his shirt cuff. 'There. Are you satisfied now?'

He stared back at Tim. 'Are you?'

'I think I am. For you finally look the way I feel. All these months you have spent, wallowing in ecstasy, or lust or guilt.' Tim made a bitter face. 'Never content unless you were torn by some emotion or other, and convinced that no one felt more deeply than you. Now, she will go. And you are all hollowed out.'

Adam nodded. He could feel the growing emptiness as she withdrew from him. A space that needed filling.

Tim smiled. 'Now imagine her with someone else.'

The pain of the thought was exquisite, for there was nothing to dull it. It was untouchable, like the phantom pains that soldiers claimed, in a limb that was no longer there. 'And this is how you feel?'

Tim nodded. 'Clarissa knows it, and she works all the harder to make me hurt. And yet I cannot leave her. She says, if I do, she will take the children, even though she cares little for them. They are innocents. They do not deserve such a mother.'

'She does not deserve to live. And if I cannot find a way to mend this?' Adam smiled. 'Then I will send her back to hell from whence she came.'

He offered his hand to his friend again, and Tim pushed it aside. 'It is a bit late for that, I think. I am going home, to my loving wife. You will understand, I trust, if the door is shut to you, should you attempt to visit.'

Adam nodded. 'As my door is now shut to you. But a word of warning. It all may get worse before it gets better. Your wife is none too happy with me. I refused her this morning. If you find letters to her, in my hand? They are old. Burn them without looking. For both our sakes.'

Tim nodded. 'Goodbye, then.' And he left him alone.

One, two, three… She'd had to start over on several occasions, for she was so angry that she kept losing her count. Penny stormed into her library and rang the bell for Jem. *Twenty-seven, twenty-eight…* And why did she even bother with it? For what good did it do to keep your temper, and be agreeable in all things, if someone you thought you could trust used your even nature against you?

Jem entered and looked at her suspiciously.

She waved an arm at the walls. 'Pack them up again.'

He squinted. 'Your Grace?'

'My books. Bring back the crates. Take them down and box them up.'

'Where will I be taking them, once I'm done?'

'I have no idea. Box them.'

'Are we going back to London, or the Scotland property that everyone talks of? Or is there somewhere…?'

'Away. I am going away, and not coming back. You were right all along. My idea was foolish, and now I am punished for it. So stop arguing with me and box these cursed books.'

'No.'

'I beg your pardon?'

He raised his voice. 'I said no, Miss Penny. I have put up with more than my share of nonsense from you over the years. But today it stops. I have carried these books halfway across England for you. You may not have noticed the fact, since you lift them one at a time. But as a group, they are heavy. And they are not moving another inch.'

'They are not remaining here,' she shouted, 'and neither am I.'

To this, Jem said nothing, merely fixed her with a long, hard look and stood, blocking the door.

'You refuse to pack the books? So be it. I'd probably

have a hard time sorting them from the ones that were already here. It is amazing how quickly one's things can get tangled with another's… But never mind that. Go to my room. I will send the maid for my dresses. They are unquestionably mine. Although I never wanted the cursed things in the first place.'

Jem showed no sign of obeying this order, either.

'What are you waiting for? Go!' She sounded shrill, even to her own ears.

Jem folded his arms.

'Look at me.' She pointed down at her clothes. 'How long has it been since I met him? A scant two months. And I no longer know myself. I dress differently. I act differently. I do not even live in the same city. I was totally content to spend days by myself. And now, if he leaves me for more than an hour or two, I miss him.

'Little by little, he has made me into exactly the thing that he wants, and now he is bored with me.'

'And for this reason, I must pack your things and carry them to you-do-not-know-where.' He remained unmoved.

'He does not love me.'

'I did not think you wished him to. When you dragged me to Scotland—'

'I was wrong.'

'And so you wish to compound the first bad decision by making another.' Jem shook his head in pity. 'I will admit, I had my doubts about the man at first. But given time, he will love you beyond reason, if he is does not already. It is hardly worth the strain on my back to bring your things down from your room, only to carry them back up again. If you insist on going, you may carry your own damn bags. Your Grace.' He added her title as an afterthought and left the room.

Chapter Twenty-Two

Penny glanced around the room, painfully aware of the silence. When had it become such a burden to be alone? It was what she had always thought she wanted.

She had been in the library for almost a week, leaving only when she was sure that the corridor was empty, to creep to her room to wash or to sleep.

But it had become harder and harder to avoid the inevitable confrontation. Most times, she could hear her husband prowling outside the library door like some kind of wild beast. On the first day, he had pounded on the oak panels, demanding that she open for him, and hear what he had to say. She feared he would shake the thing off its hinges with the force of the blows, but had put her fists to her ears, and shut her lips tight to avoid the temptation of answering him. For she knew if she saw him again, she would forget everything that had happened, and remember only how it felt to be in his arms. She would believe anything he told her, and trust any promise, no matter how false, if only he would lie with her again.

But after a day of thundering, his temper had passed like a summer storm, and the knocking had become quieter, more civilised. His shouts had turned to normal requests, 'Penny, open this door. We must speak. We cannot go on like this.'

And at last, it had come to her as a whisper. 'Penny, please...'

And now, for several days, there had been no sound at all. Just the ceaseless rustling of his footsteps on the carpet outside.

It was all foolishness. If he wanted to enter, there was nothing to stop him. He must have the key, for this was his house, not hers. If it was not in his possession, he had but to ask the servants, and they would open for him in an instant. He was the duke. He had proved often enough that he could do as he pleased.

But he did not. He respected their bargain. She had wanted privacy. And he had given this space to her. He would not cross the threshold without her permission. It was maddening. She had gotten exactly what she wanted: a library full of books and all the time in the world to enjoy them.

And yet she could not stop crying. The sight of her own books was torture, for she could not seem to concentrate long enough to read more than a few words. And those she managed all seemed to remind her of her own fate: unfaithful Odysseus and his myriad of excuses, weak will and false guilt. And Penelope, waiting for him, perpetually alone.

Why did it have to bother her so, that her husband had visited his lover? Nowhere in their original agreement, or in any of the bargaining that had occurred since, had there been any mention of his fidelity. She had not asked it of him, nor had he promised. She had held her own against the woman, for a time. But she had always known that the moment would come when she would lose. And she felt dead inside, knowing that when the mood had struck him, he would leave her to her books, as though she meant nothing to him.

And now, he thought that he could wait outside her door until her mood softened, and worm his way back into her good graces. He wanted the best of both worlds: a co-operative wife when it suited him, and his freedom all the rest of the time.

Out of the coldness in her heart rose an ember of burning rage. He had been the first to break the agreement. If he had but let her alone, she could have stayed in her study, and never have known or cared. If he had not insisted on coming to her bed, she would not be feeling jealousy over a thing that she had never wanted. If he had remained indifferent, or neglectful or at least absent, she would have viewed this liaison as just another example of his uninterest in her.

But he had treated her with kindness and respect, almost from the first. He had guarded her from ridicule and shepherded her through the maze of society, then he had touched her, and brought her more pleasure than she could have imagined possible.

And then he had taken it away. Given the chance, he would do so again. She must hold that thought foremost, and make sure it would not happen. The longer she stayed in this house, the more likely her heart would soften, and she would forget how it had felt to see Tim and her husband fighting for the attention of another. She would begin making excuses for it, and then all hope was lost.

She must leave while the anger was still fresh and she had the strength. With just the clothes on her back, if necessary. There was nothing holding her here but the fear of confronting him. Once it was done, she would be free. If he tried to stop her in the hall, she would push past without speaking. Let him follow her to her rooms. She would ignore him. She would slam the door in his face again, pack a valise and leave immediately.

She threw open the door, ready to cut him and walk by, but she almost stumbled. For he was not standing before her, but right there in the doorway, sitting on the rug with his legs drawn up to his chest, his back leaning against the frame.

She caught her hand against the wood to steady herself, and before she could stop, she had looked down into his beautiful blue eyes and felt the fight going out of her, as she feared it would. 'What on earth are you doing down there?'

He blinked up at her, surprised by her sudden appearance. 'Waiting for you to open this door. I assume you must go to your rooms at some point, but I have not been able to catch you, so I resolved to remain until you came out. I grew tired of pacing. It has been days, you know.' There was a faint accusation in his voice, as though it were somehow her fault that he was weary.

'I know exactly how long it has been.' She could feel each minute since last she had seen him. 'I would not still be here if I had managed to get my own servant to obey me. He is loyal to you, now, and will not help me move my things.'

'You really do mean to leave me, then?' At least he did not waste time in apologies that she would not have believed anyway.

'Yes.'

'I cannot say I blame you.' He looked away for a moment, sucked in a small breath and stood up. When he turned back to face her, he had become the distant, rather polite stranger she had known in London. He gestured to the library. 'May I at least come into the room? I'd prefer not to discuss this in the hall.'

As though there was a servant left in the house who was not aware of their difficulties. Perhaps he had forgotten how little effort he had made to hide them, when he had been shouting the details through the closed door. She almost smiled, before remembering how serious the situation was. She gestured through the open door and preceded him into the room.

He came through and shut it behind him. Then he turned to face her. His hands were folded behind his back like a penitent schoolboy. His mouth worked for a bit before he could find more words. 'Have you given thought as to where you will go? Not to your brother, I hope.'

It would be the logical choice. Hector would take her back. But he would never let her forget the mistake she had made in leaving. 'I do not think so.'

He nodded, obviously relieved. 'I am concerned for

your welfare, although I might not seem so. You understand that there may be a child involved as well?'

She had not thought of this fresh complication to her future. 'I will know soon enough.'

'And wherever you go, you will need space enough for your books.'

She looked at the shelves around her, and where she had seen friends before, now all she saw was dead weight. 'I doubt I will be taking them. Suddenly, it seems an awful lot of bother. And without knowing what the future holds for me…'

'No.' There was a wild light in his eyes, and he dropped his attempt at calm. The words rushed out of him. 'I can understand if you cannot abide my presence after what has happened, but do not tell me that you are abandoning your work because of me. There is a dower house on the grounds. You could stay there. The books could stay here. And you could visit as often as you liked.'

She considered how painful it would be to see him, and forced herself to look away. 'I would hardly have succeeded in escaping your influence if I were visiting this house as a guest for the majority of my days.'

'I could go from you, then.' His voice was bleak. 'You would have the books, and the space and quiet for your studies. I could go to London. I would not set foot upon the grounds without your permission. And I would be here no more than was necessary to run the estate.'

She stared at him. 'Does Clarissa approve of this plan? I imagine she would like to spend more time in London.'

'I do not know. Or care,' he added. 'It is a bit late to

tell you now. But I only went to her to say goodbye. If it troubles you still, the thought that we might meet in secret, I could travel abroad, or stay at the property in Scotland. It is farther away.'

'And you would leave the estate to me?'

'I would be honoured if you would accept it.'

She was confused. 'You love this house.'

He nodded.

'You are different, when you are here. It is where you belong.'

'You, as well. And if it can only be one of us in residence?' He smiled sadly. 'Then I wish it to be you. Without you, there would be no estate. And it is wrong that you should be banished from it for my misdeeds, or to suffer any discomfort because of my behaviour. It is my wish that you accept it from me, and anything else you might need. You are my wife. All that I have is yours.'

'That is ridiculous,' she responded. 'I never wanted all that you had. I have need of a quiet place to study. That is all.'

'And I thought I wanted nothing more than your money.'

'And a position in society. And an heir...'

He stared at the ground. 'Things have changed since the first day, have they not?'

'Yes.' She smiled sadly at the floor as well. 'Perhaps we could go back to the way we first planned.'

'I don't think that will work,' he replied.

She nodded. 'Too many things have changed.' She'd felt like a fool for even suggesting it, especially after banishing him from her life just a few days before. But when she was near to him, she remembered. And it was so hard to give him up.

'It would work fine, for a time,' he hedged. 'But I am afraid I cannot control my impulses sufficiently to keep our lives as separate as we had planned.'

Impulses? Even the thought made her temper start to rise.

One, two, three…

'Knowing I could not have you? The sight of you with other men, any other man, even if it was quite innocent, or you were very discreet, would drive me mad with jealousy.'

Four, five… 'What?'

He continued, ignoring the interruption. 'Before we came to Wales, I thought if I could keep you all to myself, then you would forget anyone but me. I am sorry.'

'And you did not tell me that we were neighbors to the Coltons?'

'Because I did not want you to see them. Especially not Tim, for I did not think I could trust him, given all that has happened. If the world were different, and we were all free, you would have done better to choose him, for his temperament would suit you.'

Adam's face darkened and his lips twisted in a bitter smile. 'But I find that I do not care, when you are near, what is best for you or that you deserve better. You are mine, and I want to keep you all to myself.' His smile softened as he remembered. 'It was so good, being alone with you. And you seemed content with just me for company.'

'But what about Clarissa?' She held her breath.

'The day I went to her, she sent me a letter, saying that if I would not come to her, she would come here. It would have ruined everything.' He looked up, and his face was blank. 'It wouldn't have mattered. Things are ruined, in any case. There will be less bother, now that Tim and I are quits. I will not need to pretend civility with her. She is angry, and promises to make a scandal. There are letters that I wrote to her.'

He rubbed his hand over his eyes, as though to blot out the memory. 'They are very detailed. And I would ask you, as a last favour, to destroy them without reading them should they come your way. The words are no longer true, but to read them might cause you pain.

'But if she does not send them to you, then she will circulate them freely in London next Season. You may be more comfortable if you remain here, far from the gossip of the *ton*. I am sorry, but whatever might happen, you should know and prepare yourself. Perhaps it will not matter and she will be quiet, now that she sees we are…apart.' The last word seemed to come difficult to him.

'It will not matter to your position, of course. You are Duchess of Bellston for as long as you wish to be. Nothing anyone says will change that. But people will talk. I am afraid you will find it embarrassing.' He said it as gently as possible, and his face was full of remorse.

The idea of talk, which would have appalled her a few weeks before, seemed distant and unimportant. What did it matter what people said? Nothing could hurt as bad as being without Adam. 'It does not really matter, does it, if it is all in the past? It is not as if you can change what you did, even if it was very awful.'

He looked hopeful, for a moment, and pulled one of the straight-backed library chairs to him, and sat a respectful distance from her.

'I know it is too late to say these things. But I would do anything to take back what has happened. I never wanted anything less for you than you wanted for yourself: peace and security. That you might come to harm from behaviours of mine, things that occurred long before you knew me—it pains me more than you can imagine. And if I had known, the day we met, that I would make you unhappy, I swear I'd never have married you.'

She shrugged. 'You can have no idea what you might have done, for I dare say you had little control of yourself on that particular occasion.'

'I still cannot remember the details,' he admitted. 'Only that I was convinced you were sent by God to lead me to salvation. I'd have followed you to the ends of the earth. And still would, if you would but allow it. You have brought me more happiness than I deserve.'

'I made you happy,' she repeated numbly.

He smiled and shook his head in disbelief. 'You did not realise it? Yes, you made me happy. You are unlike any woman I have ever met. Blazingly intelligent, unfailingly honest, and a rock to which I can cling in moments of turmoil. And when we are together as man and wife?' He shook his head again. 'I never knew how it felt to join in love, until you came to me.'

'Love?' she whispered.

He nodded. 'I love you, Penelope. I cannot help myself. It is not what you wanted, of course. Not peaceful or quiet at all, for neither of those virtues are in my nature. But there it is.'

He loved her. What an amazing idea. She felt the warmth of the words against her heart, growing in her, surrounding her to keep her safe, and heating her blood in a way that was not safe at all, but just as wonderful.

'And you were faithful to me,' she said, testing.

'Strangely enough, yes. I put off my mistress, I forsook my old haunts. There has been no one but you since the day we met. What Tim saw when he spied me with Clarissa was no doing of mine.'

She stepped closer and reached out a hand to him, touching his hair, and trailing her fingers slowly down his cheek. He closed his eyes for a moment, then turned his head to press kisses into her palm, seizing her hand in his so that she could not pull away.

And she felt the familiar thrill of power at the sight of him, cradling her hand as though he feared the loss of her touch. He kissed her knuckles again, and bowed his head to her. 'My fate is yours to decide, Penny. I will do as you wish in all things. I will go tonight, if you say I must. But I beg you, do not be apart from me, for I fear I shall go mad with the loss of you.'

Fierce joy was rushing through her, and desire mingled with it. And without speaking, she touched him under the chin, urging his lips up to hers and kissing slowly into his open mouth.

His breath trembled for a moment, and then his response was eager, hungry to deepen the kiss.

She pulled away, and he looked up with hope, awaiting her answer, and she looked into his eyes, and saw only herself reflected back.

When she spoke, she was pleased that her voice sounded cool, collected and very much like the ladies of the *ton* that had once beguiled her husband and not at all like she truly was: too far gone with love of him to ever leave. 'So you love me, and wish to give me all that I might desire?'

He gave the barest nod, but his eyes sparkled with shared devilment.

She reached to his throat, and undid the knot of his cravat, tugging him up out of his chair. 'Then, we have much to discuss. But first, you must give me my garter back.'

* * * * *

Aella closed her eyes and sensed a distinct shift, like movement from the world around her to the unseen world.

She opened her eyes. And had a slight shock at the man standing ten feet away. He wasn't just any man. Her heart leaped and pounded. He reminded her of a fierce warrior from an ancient civilization. Incan? She wasn't sure but she felt his deep power and masculinity.

I'm Aella. Are you the guardian of this sacred site? she asked, hoping her telepathy was strong.

Fox's entire body soared with joy. Fox struggled to put his personal pleasure aside.

Greetings, Aella. I'm the assistant guardian to this sacred area. You may call me Fox. How can I be of service to you, Aella? he asked.

I'm searching for a green sphere. A legend says that the Emperor Pachacuti had seven emerald spheres created for the Emerald Key necklace. He had seven of his priestesses and priests travel the world to hide these spheres from evil forces. It is said that when all seven spheres are found, restrung and worn, that Light will return to the Earth. The fourth sphere is here, at your sacred site. Are you aware of it? Aella held her breath. She loved looking at him, especially his sensual mouth. The desire to kiss him came out of nowhere.

Fox was stunned by the request. *I know of the Emerald Key necklace because I served the emperor at the time it was created. However, I did not realize that one of the spheres is here.*

Aella felt sad. Why? Every time she looked at Fox, her heart felt as if it would tear out of her chest. *May I stay in touch with you as I work with this site?* she asked.

Of course. Fox wanted nothing more than to be here with her. To absorb her ephemeral beauty and hear her speak once more.

Aella's spirit lifted. What *was* this strange connection between them? Her curiosity was strong, but she had more pressing matters. In the next few days, Aella knew her life would change forever. How, she had no idea….

Look for REUNION
by USA TODAY *bestselling author*
Lindsay McKenna,
available April 2010, only
from Silhouette® Nocturne™.